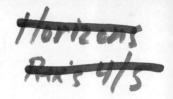

THIS BOOK
BELONGS TO:

_____

THE DEEP WOODS

THE TWILIGHT WOODS

THE EDGELANDS

The Edge.

The Edge CHRONICLES

BEYOND THE DEEPWOODS

Paul Stewart
&
Chris Riddell

David Fickling Books
OXFORD · NEW YORK

A DAVID FICKLING BOOK

Published by David Fickling Books
an imprint of Random House Children's Books
a division of Random House, Inc.
New York

Originally published in Great Britain by Doubleday, an imprint of
Random House Children's Books.

www.randomhouse.com/kids
www.edgechronicles.com

Library of Congress Cataloging-in-Publication Data
is available upon request
ISBN-10: 0-385-75068-4 (trade)—ISBN-10: 0-385-75069-2 (lib. bdg.)
ISBN-13: 978-0-385-75068-4 (trade)—ISBN-13: 978-0-385-75069-1 (lib. bdg.)
Printed in the United States of America
June 2004
20 19 18 17 16 15 14 13
First American Edition

For Joseph and William

BEYOND THE
DEEPWOODS

·INTRODUCTION·

Far far away, jutting out into the emptiness beyond, like the figurehead of a mighty stone ship, is the Edge. A torrent of water pours endlessly over the lip of rock at its overhanging point.

The river here is broad and swollen, and roars as it hurls itself down into the swirling, misty void below. It is difficult to believe that the river – like everything else that is large and loud and full of its own importance – might ever have been any different. Yet the origins of the Edgewater River could scarcely be humbler.

Its source lies far back inland, high up in the dark and forbidding Deepwoods. It is a small, bubbling pool, which spills over as a trickle and down along a bed of sandy gravel, little wider than a piece of rope. Its insignificance is multiplied a thousandfold by the grandeur of the Deepwoods themselves.

Dark and deeply mysterious, the Deepwoods is a harsh and perilous place for those who call it home. And there are many who do. Woodtrolls, slaughterers, gyle goblins, termagant trogs: countless tribes and strange groupings scratch a living in the dappled sunlight and moonglow beneath its lofty canopy.

It is a hard life and one fraught with many dangers – monstrous creatures, flesh-eating trees, marauding hordes of ferocious beasts, both large and small . . . Yet it can also be profitable, for the succulent fruits and buoyant woods which grow there are highly valued. Sky pirates and merchant Leagues-men vie for trade, and battle it out with one another high up above the endless ocean-green treetops.

Where the clouds descend, there lie the Edgelands, a barren wasteland of swirling mists, spirits and night-mares. Those who lose themselves in the Edgelands face one of two possible fates. The lucky ones will stumble blindly to the cliff edge and plunge to their deaths. The unlucky ones will find themselves in the Twilight Woods.

Bathed in their neverending golden half-light, the Twilight Woods are enchanting, but they are also treach-erous. The atmosphere there is heady, intoxicating. Those who breathe it for too long forget the reason they ever came to the Twilight Woods, like the lost knights on long-forgotten quests, who would give up on life – if only life would give up on them.

On occasions, the heavy stillness is disturbed by viol-ent storms which blow in from beyond the Edge. Drawn to the Twilight Woods, like iron filings to a magnet, like moths to a flame, the storms circle the glowing sky – sometimes for days at a time. Some of the storms are special. The lightning bolts they release create storm-phrax, a substance so valuable that it too – despite the awful dangers of the Twilight Woods – acts like a magnet, like a flame, to those who would possess it.

At its lower reaches, the Twilight Woods give way to the Mire. It is a stinking, polluted place, rank with the slurry from the factories and foundries of Undertown which have pumped and dumped their waste so long that the land is dead. And yet – like everywhere else on the Edge – there are those who live here. Pink-eyed and bleached as white as their surroundings, they are the rummagers, the scavengers. A few serve as guides, steering their charges across the desolate landscape of poisonous blow-holes and sinking mud, before robbing them blind and abandoning them to their fate.

Those who do make their way across the Mire find themselves in a warren of ramshackle hovels and run-down slums which straddles the oozing Edgewater River. This is Undertown.

Its population is made up of all the strange peoples, creatures and tribes of the Edgeworld crammed into its narrow alleys. It is dirty, over-crowded and often violent, yet Undertown is also the centre of all economic activity – both above-board and underhand. It buzzes, it bustles, it bristles with energy. Everyone who lives there has a particular trade, with its attendant league and clearly defined district. This leads to intrigue, plotting, bitter competition and perpetual disputes – district with district, league with league, tradesman with rival tradesman. The only matter which unites all those in the League of

Free Merchants is their shared fear and hatred of the sky pirates who dominate the skies above the Edge in their independent boats and prey off any hapless merchant-men whose paths they cross.

At the centre of Undertown is a great iron ring, to which a long and heavy chain – now taut, now slack – extends up into the sky. At its end, is a great floating rock.

Like all the other buoyant rocks of the Edge, it started out in the Stone Gardens – poking up out of the ground, growing, being pushed up further by new rocks growing beneath it, and becoming bigger still. The chain was attached when the rock became large and light enough to float up into the sky. Upon it, the magnificent city of Sanctaphrax has been constructed.

Sanctaphrax, with its tall thin towers connected by viaducts and walkways, is a seat of learning. It is peopled with academics, alchemists and apprentices and furnished with libraries, laboratories and lecture halls, refectories and common rooms. The subjects studied there are as obscure as they are jealously guarded and, despite the apparent air of fusty, bookish benevolence, Sanctaphrax is a seething cauldron of rivalries, plot and counter-plot, and bitter faction-fighting.

The Deepwoods, the Edgelands, the Twilight Woods, the Mire and the Stone Gardens. Undertown and Sanctaphrax. The River Edgewater. Names on a map.

Yet behind each name lie a thousand tales – tales that have been recorded in ancient scrolls, tales that have been passed down the generations by word of mouth – tales which even now are being told.

What follows is but one of those tales.

CHAPTER ONE

THE SNATCHWOOD CABIN

Twig sat on the floor between his mother's knees, and curled his toes in the thick fleece of the tilder rug. It was cold and draughty in the cabin. Twig leaned forwards and opened the door of the stove.

'I want to tell you the story of how you got your name,' his mother said.

'But I know that story, Mother-Mine,' Twig protested.

Spelda sighed. Twig felt her warm breath on the back of his neck, and smelled the pickled tripweed she had eaten for lunch. He wrinkled his nose. Like so much of the food which the woodtrolls relished, Twig found tripweed disgusting, particularly pickled. It was slimy and smelled of rotten eggs.

'This time it will be a little different,' he heard his mother saying. 'This time I will finish the tale.'

Twig frowned. 'I thought I'd already heard the ending.'

7

Spelda tousled her son's thick black hair. He's grown so fast, she thought, and wiped a tear from the end of her rubbery button-nose. 'A tale can have many endings,' she said sadly, and watched the purple light from the fire gleaming on Twig's high cheekbones and sharp chin. 'From the moment you were born,' she began, as she always began, 'you were different . . .'

Twig nodded. It had been painful, so painful, being *different* when he was growing up. Yet it amused him now to think of his parents' surprise when he had appeared: dark, green-eyed, smooth-skinned, and already with unusually long legs for a woodtroll. He stared into the fire.

The lufwood was burning very well. Purple flames blazed all round the stubby logs as they bumped and tumbled around inside the stove.

The woodtrolls had many types of wood to choose from and each had its own special properties. Scentwood, for instance, burned with a fragrance that sent those who breathed it drifting into a dream-filled sleep, while wood from the silvery-turquoise lullabee tree sang as the flames lapped at its bark – strange mournful songs, they were, and not at all to everyone's taste. And then there was the bloodoak, complete with its parasitic sidekick, a barbed creeper known as tarry vine.

Obtaining bloodoak wood was hazardous. Any woodtroll who did not know his woodlore was liable to end up satisfying the tree's love of flesh – for the blood-oak and the tarry vine were two of the greatest dangers in the dark and perilous Deepwoods.

Certainly the wood of the bloodoak gave off a lot of heat, and it neither smelled nor sang, but the way it wailed and screamed as it burned put off all but a few. No, among the woodtrolls, lufwood was by far the most popular. It burned well and they found its purple glow restful.

Twig yawned as Spelda continued her story. Her voice was high-pitched but guttural; it seemed to gurgle in the back of her throat.

'At four months you were already walking upright,' she was saying, and Twig heard the pride in his mother's words. Most woodtroll children remained down on their knuckles until they were at least eighteen months old.

'*But* . . .' Twig whispered softly. Drawn back inside the story despite himself, he was already anticipating the next part. It was time for the 'but'. Every time it arrived Twig would shudder and hold his breath.

'But,' she said, 'although you were so ahead of the others physically, you would not speak. Three years old you were, and not a single word!' She shifted round in her chair. 'And I don't have to tell you how serious *that* can be!'

Once again his mother sighed. Once again Twig screwed up his face in disgust. Something Taghair had once said came back to him: 'Your nose knows where you belong.' Twig had taken it to mean that he would always recognize the unique smell of his own home. But what if he was wrong? What if the wise old oakelf had been saying – in his usual roundabout way – that because his nose didn't like what it smelled, this was *not* his home?

Twig swallowed guiltily. This was something he had wished so often as he'd lain in his bunk after yet another day of being teased and taunted and bullied.

Through the window, the sun was sinking lower in the dappled sky. The zigzag silhouettes of the Deepwood pines were glinting like frozen bolts of lightning. Twig knew there would be snow before his father returned that night.

He thought of Tuntum, out there in the Deepwoods far beyond the anchor tree. Perhaps at that very moment he was sinking his axe into the trunk of a bloodoak. Twig shuddered. His father's felling tales had filled him with deep horror on many a howling night. Although he was a master carver, Tuntum Snatchwood earned most of his money from the illicit repair of the sky pirates' ships. This meant using buoyant wood – and the most buoyant wood of all was bloodoak.

Twig was uncertain of his father's feelings towards him. Whenever Twig returned to the cabin with a blood-ied nose or blacked eyes or clothes covered in slung mud, he wanted his father to wrap him up in his arms and soothe the pain away. Instead, Tuntum would give him advice and make demands.

'Bloody *their* noses,' he said once. 'Black *their* eyes. And throw not mud but *dung*! Show them what you're made of.'

Later, when his mother was smoothing hyleberry salve onto his bruises, she would explain that Tuntum was only concerned to prepare him for the harshness of the world outside. But Twig was unconvinced. It was not concern he had seen in Tuntum's eyes but contempt.

Twig absent-mindedly wound a strand of his long, dark hair round and round his finger as Spelda went on with her story.

'Names,' she was saying. 'Where would we woodtrolls be without them? They tame the wild things of the Deepwoods, and give us our own identity. Ne'er sip of a nameless soup, as the saying goes. Oh, Twig, how I fretted when, at three years old, you were still without a name.'

Twig shivered. He knew that any woodtroll who died without a name would be doomed to an eternity in open sky. The trouble was that until an infant had uttered its first word the naming ritual could not take place.

'Was I really so silent, Mother-Mine?' said Twig.

Spelda looked away. 'Not a single word passed your lips. I thought perhaps you were like your great-grandfather Weezil. He never spoke either.' She sighed. 'So on your third birthday, I decided to perform the ritual anyway. I . . .'

'Did great-grandfather Weezil look like me?' Twig interrupted.

'No, Twig,' said Spelda. 'There has never been a Snatchwood – nor any other woodtroll – who has ever looked like you.'

Twig tugged at the twist of hair. 'Am I ugly?' he said.

Spelda chuckled. As she did so, her downy cheeks puffed out and her small charcoal-grey eyes disappeared in folds of leathery skin. '*I* don't think so,' she said. She leaned forwards and wrapped her long arms around Twig's chest. 'You'll always be my beautiful boy.' She paused. 'Now, where was I?'

'The naming ritual,' Twig reminded her.

He had heard the story so often, he was no longer sure what he could remember and what he had been told. As the sun rose, Spelda had taken the well-worn path which led to the anchor tree. There she tethered herself to its bulky trunk and set off into the dark woods. This was dangerous, not only because of the unseen perils that lurked in the Deepwoods but because there was always the chance that the rope would snag and break. Woodtrolls' deepest terror was being lost.

Those who did stray from the path and lose their way were vulnerable to attacks from the gloamglozer – the wildest of all the wild creatures in the Deepwoods. Every woodtroll lived in constant terror of an encounter with the fearsome beast. Spelda herself had often frightened her older children with tales of the forest bogeyman: 'If you don't stop being such a naughty woodtroll,' she would say, 'the gloamglozer will get you!'

Deeper and deeper into the Deepwoods, Spelda went. All round her the forest echoed with howls and shrieks of concealed beasts. She fingered the amulets and lucky charms around her neck, and prayed for a swift and safe return.

Finally getting to the end of her tether, Spelda pulled a knife – a *naming* knife – from her belt. The knife was important. It had been made especially for her son, as knives were made for all the woodtroll children. They were essential for the naming ritual and, when the youngsters came of age, each one was given his or her individual naming knife to keep.

Spelda gripped the handle tightly, reached forwards and, as the procedure demanded, hacked off a piece of wood from the nearest tree. It was this little bit of Deepwood which would reveal her child's name.

Spelda worked quickly. She knew only too well that the sound of chopping would attract inquisitive, possibly deadly, attention. When she was done she tucked the wood under her arm, trotted back through the woods, untied herself from the anchor tree, and returned to the cabin. There she kissed the piece of wood twice and threw it into the fire.

'With your brothers and sisters, the names came at once,' Spelda explained. 'Snodpill, Henchweed, Poohsniff; as clear as you like. But with you the wood did nothing but crackle and hiss. The Deepwoods had refused to name you.'

'And yet I have a name,' said Twig.

'Indeed you have,' said Spelda. 'Thanks to Taghair.'

Twig nodded. He remembered the occasion so well. Taghair had just returned to the village after a long spell away. Twig remembered how overjoyed the woodtrolls had all been to have the oakelf back among them. For Taghair, who was well versed in the finer points of woodlore, was their adviser, their counsellor, their oracle. It was to him that the woodtrolls came with their worries.

'There was already quite a gathering beneath his ancient lullabee tree when we arrived,' Spelda was saying. 'Taghair was sitting in his empty caterbird cocoon, holding forth about where he had been and what he had seen on his travels. The moment he saw me, however, his eyes opened wide and his ears rotated. "Whatever's up?" he asked.

'And I told him. I told him everything. "Oh, for good-ness sake, pull yourself together," he said. Then he pointed to you. "Tell me," he said. "What is that round the little one's neck?"

'"That's his comfort cloth," I said. "He won't let any-one touch it. And he won't be parted from it neither. His father tried once – said the boy was too old for such childish things. But he just curled up into a ball and cried and cried till we gave it back to him."'

Twig knew what was coming next. He had heard it so many times before.

'Then Taghair said, "Give it to me," and stared into your eyes with those big black eyes of his – all oakelves have eyes like that. They can see those parts of the world that remain hidden to others.'

'And I gave him my comfort cloth,' whispered Twig. Even now he didn't like anyone touching it, and kept it tightly knotted around his neck.

'That you did,' continued Spelda. 'And I can scarce believe it to this day. But that wasn't all, oh, no.'

'Oh, no,' echoed Twig.

'He took your cloth and he sort of stroked it, all gentle like, as if it was a living thing, and then he traced the pattern on it with his fingertip, ever so lightly. 'A lullabee tree,' he said at last, and I saw that he was right. I'd always thought it was just a pretty pattern – all those squiggles and little stitches – but no, it was a lullabee tree all right, plain as the nose on your face.'

Twig laughed.

'And the strange thing was, you didn't mind old

Taghair touching your cloth. You just sat there, all serious and silent. Then he gave you that stare of his again and said in a soft voice, "You're part of the Deepwoods, silent one. The naming ritual has not worked, but you are a part of the Deepwoods . . . A part of the Deepwoods," he repeated, his eyes glazing over. Then he raised his head and spread wide his arms. "His name shall be . . ."'

'. . . Twig!' Twig exclaimed, unable to keep silent a moment longer.

'That's right,' said Spelda, laughing. 'Out you came with it, just like that. Twig! The first word you ever spoke. And then Taghair said, "You must look after him well, for the boy is special."'

Not *different*, but *special*! It was the one fact that had kept him going when the other woodtroll children had picked on him so mercilessly. Not a single day had passed without some incident or other. But the worst time of all was when he'd been set upon during the fateful trockbladder match.

Before then, Twig had loved the game. Not that he was very good at it, but he had always enjoyed the excitement of the chase – for trockbladder was a game that involved a great deal of running about.

It was played on a large square of land between the back of the village and the forest. The pitch was crisscrossed with well-worn paths beaten out by generations of young woodtrolls. Between these bare tracks, the grass grew thick and tall.

The rules of the game were simple. There were two teams, with as many woodtrolls on each side as wanted to play. The aim was to catch the trockbladder – the bladder of a hammelhorn stuffed with dried trockbeans – and run twelve paces, calling out the numbers as you went. If you managed that, you were allowed a shot at the central basket, which could double your score. However, since the ground was often slippery, the trockbladder always squidgy, and the entire opposing team was trying to wrest the ball away, this was not as easy as it sounded. In his eight years of playing the game, Twig had never once managed to score a trockbladder.

On this particular morning, no-one was having much luck. Heavy rain had left the pitch waterlogged and the game kept stopping and starting as, time after time, woodtroll after woodtroll came sliding off the muddy paths.

It wasn't until the third quarter that the trockbladder landed near enough to Twig for him to seize it and start running. 'ONE, TWO, THREE . . .' he yelled out as, with the trockbladder wedged beneath the elbow of his left arm, he belted along the paths which led to the centre of the pitch. The nearer to the basket you were when you reached twelve, the easier it was to score.

'FOUR, FIVE . . .' In front of him half-a-dozen members of the opposing team were converging on him. He

darted down a path to the left. His opponents chased after him.

'SIX, SEVEN . . .'

'To me! Twig, to me!' various members of his own team called out. 'Pass it!'

But Twig didn't pass it. He wanted to score. He wanted to hear his team-mates' cheers, to feel their hands slapping him on the back. For once, he wanted to be the hero.

'EIGHT, NINE . . .'

He was completely surrounded.

'PASS IT TO ME!' he heard. It was Hoddergruff, calling from the far side of the pitch. Twig knew that if he chucked the ball to him now his friend would have a good chance of scoring for the team. But that was no good. You remembered who scored, not who set the goal up. Twig wanted everyone to remember that *he* had scored.

He paused. Half of the opposing team were almost upon him. He couldn't go forwards. He couldn't go back. He looked round at the basket. So near and yet so far, and he wanted that goal. He wanted it more than anything.

All at once, a little voice in his head seemed to say, 'But what's the problem? The rules say nothing about sticking to the path.' Twig looked back towards the basket, and swallowed nervously. The next instant he did what no woodtroll before had ever done: *he left the path.* The long grass whipped at his bare legs as he loped towards the basket.

'TEN, ELEVEN . . . TWELVE!' he screamed, and dunked the bladder down through the basket. 'A trockbladder!' he cried, and looked round happily. 'A twenty-four pointer. I've scored a tro . . .' He stopped. The woodtrolls on both teams were glaring at him. There were no cheers. No slaps on the back.

'You stepped from the path!' one of them shouted.

'*No-one* steps from the path,' cried another.

'But . . . but . . .' Twig stammered. 'There's nothing in the rules that says . . .'

But the other woodtrolls were not listening. They knew, of course, that the rules didn't mention keeping to

22

the paths – but then why should they? In trockbladder, as in their lives, the woodtrolls never *ever* strayed from the paths. It was a given. It was taken as read. It would have made as much sense to have a rule telling them not to stop breathing!

All at once, as if by some pre-arranged signal, the woodtrolls fell on Twig. 'You lanky weirdo,' they cried as they kicked him and punched him. 'You hideous gangly freak!'

A sudden fiery pain tore through Twig's arm. It felt as if it had been branded. He looked up to see a wodge of his smooth flesh being viciously twisted by a handful of hard spatula-fingers.

'Hoddergruff,' Twig whispered.

The Snatchwoods and the Gropeknots were neighbours. He and Hoddergruff had been born within a week of each other, and grew up together. Twig had thought they were friends. Hoddergruff sneered, and twisted the skin round still further. Twig bit into his lower lip and fought back the tears. Not because of the pain in his arm – that he could bear – but because Hoddergruff had now also turned against him.

As Twig had stumbled home, battered, bruised and bleeding, it was the fact that he'd lost his only friend that hurt most. Now, because he was different, he was also alone.

*

'*Special!*' said Twig, and snorted.

'Yes,' said Spelda. 'Even the sky pirates recognized that fact when they saw you,' she added softly. 'That is why your father . . .' Her voice faltered. 'Why we . . . That is why you must leave home.'

Twig froze. Leave home? What did she mean? He spun round and stared at his mother. She was weeping.

'I don't understand,' he said. 'Do you want me to go?'

'Of course I don't, Twig,' she sobbed. 'But you'll be thirteen in less than a week. An adult. What will you do then? You cannot fell wood like your father. You . . . you're not built for it. And where will you live? The cabin is already too small for you. And now that the sky pirates know about you . . .'

Twig twisted the knot of hair round and round his finger. Three weeks earlier he had gone with his father

24

far into the Deepwoods, where woodtrolls felled and fashioned the wood that they sold to the sky pirates.

Whereas his father could walk upright beneath the lowest branches, Twig had had to stoop. And even that wasn't enough. Time and again he knocked his head, until his scalp had become a mass of angry red grazes. In the end Twig had had no option but to crawl on his hands and knees to the clear-ing.

'Our latest felling recruit,' Tuntum had said to the sky pirate in charge of delivery that morning.

The pirate glanced over his clipboard and looked Twig up and down. 'Looks too tall,' he said, and went back to his paperwork.

Twig stared at the sky pirate. Tall and upright, he looked magnificent with his tricorn hat and tooled leather breast-plate, his parawings and waxed side-whiskers. His coat was patched in places but was, with its ruffs, tassles, golden buttons and braid, none the less splendid for that. Each of the numerous objects that hung from special hooks seemed to shout of adventure.

Twig found himself wondering who the sky pirate had fought with that cutlass, with its ornately jewelled hilt – and what had caused the nick in its long curved blade. He wondered what marvels the sky pirate had seen through his telescope, what walls he had scaled with the grappling irons, what distant places his compass had led him to.

Suddenly, the sky pirate looked up again. He caught Twig staring at him and raised a quizzical brow. Twig stared at his feet. 'Tell you what,' the sky pirate said to Tuntum. 'There's always a place for a tall young man on a sky ship.'

'No,' said Tuntum sharply. 'Thank you very much for the offer,' he added politely. 'But, no.'

Tuntum knew his son wouldn't last ten minutes on board ship. The sky pirates were shiftless, shameless rogues. They would slit your throat as soon as look at you. It was only because they paid so well for the buoyant Deepwood timber that the woodtrolls had anything to do with them at all.

The sky pirate shrugged. 'Just a thought,' he said, and turned away. 'Pity, though,' he muttered.

As Twig crawled back through the Deepwoods behind his father, he thought of the ships he had watched flying overhead, sails full, soaring off, up and away. 'Skyriding,' he whispered, and his heart quickened. Surely, he thought, there are worse things to do.

Back in the woodtroll cabin, Spelda thought otherwise. 'Oh those sky pirates!' she grumbled. 'Tuntum should never have taken you to meet them in the first place. Now they'll be back for you, as sure as my name's Spelda Snatchwood.'

'But the sky pirate I saw didn't seem bothered whether I joined the crew, or not,' said Twig.

'That's what they pretend,' said Spelda. 'But look what happened to Hobblebark and Hogwort. Seized from their beds they were, and never seen again. Oh, Twig, I couldn't bear it if that happened to you. It would break my heart.'

Outside, the wind howled through the dense Deepwoods. As darkness fell, the air was filled with the sounds of the wakening night creatures. Fromps coughed and spat, quarms squealed, while the great banderbear beat its monstrous hairy chest and yodelled to its mate. Far away in the distance Twig could just make out the familiar rhythmical pounding of the slaughterers, still hard at work.

'What am I to do, then?' Twig asked softly.

Spelda sniffed. 'In the short term, you're to go and

stay with Cousin Snetterbark,' she said. 'We've already sent message, and he's expecting you. Just until things blow over,' she added. 'Sky willing, you'll be safe there.'

'And *after*,' said Twig. 'I can come home again then, can I?'

'Yes,' said Spelda slowly. Twig knew at once that there was more to come.

'But?' he said.

Spelda trembled and hugged the boy's head to her chest. 'Oh, Twig, my beautiful boy,' she sobbed. 'There is something else I must tell you.'

Twig pulled away and looked up at her troubled face. There were tears rolling down his own cheeks now. 'What is it, Mother-Mine?' he asked nervously.

'Oh, Gloamglozer!' Spelda cursed. 'This isn't easy.' She looked at the boy tearfully. 'Although I have loved you as my own since the day you arrived, you are not my son, Twig. Nor is Tuntum your father.'

Twig stared in silent disbelief. 'Then, who am I?' he said.

Spelda shrugged. 'We found you,' she said. 'A little bundle, all wrapped up in a shawl, at the foot of our tree.'

'*Found* me,' Twig whispered.

Spelda nodded, leaned forwards and touched the cloth knotted at Twig's neck. Twig flinched.

'My comfort cloth?' he said. 'The shawl?'

Spelda sighed. 'The very same,' she said. 'The shawl we found you wrapped in. The shawl you won't be parted from, even now.'

Twig stroked the fabric with trembling fingers. He heard Spelda sniff.

'Oh, Twig,' she said. 'Although we are not your parents, Tuntum and I have loved you like our very own. Tuntum asked me to say ... goodbye for him. He said ...' She stopped, overwhelmed with sadness. 'He said to tell you that ... that, whatever happens, you must never forget ... he loves you.'

Now that the words were said, Spelda abandoned herself to her grief completely. She wailed with misery, and uncontrolled sobbing racked her entire body.

Twig knelt across and wrapped his arms right round his mother's back. 'So I am to leave at once,' he said.

'It's for the best,' Spelda said. 'But you will return, Twig. Won't you?' she added uncertainly. 'Believe me, my beautiful boy, I didn't ever want to have to tell you the end of the tale, but ...'

'Don't cry,' said Twig. 'This *isn't* the end of the tale.'

Spelda looked up and sniffed. 'You're right,' she said, and smiled bravely. 'It's more of a beginning, isn't it? Yes, that's what it is, Twig. A new start.'

.CHAPTER TWO.

THE HOVER WORM

The sounds of the Deepwoods echoed loudly all round as Twig walked along the path through the trees. He shivered, tightened his scarf and pulled up the collar of his leather jacket.

He hadn't wanted to leave that evening at all. It was dark and cold. But Spelda had been insistent. 'There's no time like the present,' she'd said several times as she got together the bits and pieces that Twig would need for his journey: a leather bottle, a rope, a small bag of food and – most precious of all – his naming knife. Twig had finally come of age.

'Anyway, you know what they say,' she added, as she reached up and tied two wooden charms around her son's neck. 'Depart by night, arrive by day.'

Twig knew Spelda had been putting on a brave face. 'But be careful,' she insisted. 'It's dark out there and I know what you're like, forever dreaming and dawdling and wondering what's round the next corner.'

'Yes, mother,' said Twig.

'And don't "yes, mother" me,' said Spelda. 'This is important. Remember, stick to the path if you want to steer clear of the fearsome gloamglozer. We woodtrolls *always* stick to the path.'

'But I'm not a woodtroll,' mumbled Twig, tears stinging his eyes.

'You're my little boy,' said Spelda, hugging him tightly. 'Stick to the path. Woodtrolls know best. Now, be off with you, and give my love to Cousin Snetterbark. You'll be back before you know it. Everything will be back to normal. You'll see . . .'

Spelda couldn't finish. The tears were coming thick and fast. Twig turned and set off down the shadowy path into the gloom.

Normal! he thought. *Normal!* I don't want things to be normal. Normal is trockbladder games. Normal is felling trees. Normal is always being left out, never belonging. And why should it be any different at Cousin Snetterbark's?

Being pressganged into crewing a sky ship suddenly seemed more appealing than ever. The sky pirates roamed the skies above the Deepwoods. Surely their airborne adventures must be better than anything down here on the forest floor.

A desperate howl of pain echoed through the trees. For a second, the Deepwoods were still. The next second the night sounds returned, louder than before, as if each and every creature was rejoicing that *it* was not the one who had fallen prey to some hungry predator.

As he walked on, Twig began putting names to the creatures he could hear out there in the treacherous Deepwoods, away from the path. It helped to calm his pounding heart. There were squealing quarms and coughing fromps in the trees above his head. Neither of them could harm a woodtroll – at least, not fatally. Away to his right, he heard the chattering screech of a razorflit, about to dive. The next instant, the air was filled with the scream of its victim: a woodrat, perhaps, or a leafgobbler.

Some way further on, with the dark path still stretching out in front of him, the forest opened up. Twig stopped and stared at the silver moonlight that snaked along the trunks and branches, and gleamed on the waxy leaves. This was the first time he had been out in the forest after dark, and it was beautiful – more beautiful than he had ever imagined.

With his eyes gazing up at the silvery leaves, Twig took a step forward, away from the shadowy path. The moonlight bathed him in its cold glow and made his skin shine like metal. His billowing breath gleamed, snow-bright.

'In-*cred*-ible,' said Twig, and took a couple of steps more.

Below his feet, the glittering frost cracked and crunched. Icicles hung down from a weeping-willoak, and the beads of liquid on a dewdrop tree had frosted and frozen, and glistened now like pearls. A wispy sapling with fronds like hair swayed in the icy breeze.

'A-*maz*-ing,' said Twig, as he wandered on. Now left. Now right. Now round a corner. Now over a slope. It was all so mysterious, all so new.

He stopped by a bank of quivering plants with tall spiky leaves and budded stems, all glinting in the moonlight. All at once, the buds began to pop open. One by one. Until the bank was covered with massive round flowers – with petals like shavings of ice – that turned their heads to the moon, and glowed with its brilliance.

Twig smiled to himself and turned away. 'Just a *weeny* bit further . . .' he said.

A tumblebush tumbled past him and disappeared into the shadows. Moonbells and tinkleberries jingled and jangled in the gathering wind.

Then Twig heard another noise. He spun round. A small, sleek, furry brown creature with a corkscrew tail scurried across the forest floor, squeaking with terror.

The screech of a woodowl sliced through the air.

Twig's heart began to race. He looked round him wildly. There were eyes in the shadows. Yellow eyes. Green eyes. Red eyes. And all of them staring at him. 'Oh, no,' he moaned. 'What have I *done*?'

Twig knew what he had done. 'Never stray from the path,' Spelda had said. Yet that was *precisely* what he had done. Entranced by the silvery beauty of the Deepwoods, he had strayed from the safety of the path.

Twig groaned. 'I can't do anything right! Stupid! Stupid! Stupid!' he shouted at himself, as he stumbled this way and that, desperately trying to find his way back to the path. 'STU—'

All at once he heard something; a sound which silenced his voice and froze him to the spot. It was the wheezing pant of a halitoad – a huge and dangerous reptile, with breath so foul it could stun its victim at twenty paces. At ten paces the stench was lethal. A single evil-smelling belch had been enough to kill Hoddergruff's uncle.

What could he do? Where could he go? Twig had never been away from the Deepwoods paths on his own before. He started this way, stopped, ran the other way, and stopped again. The sound of the wheezing halitoad seemed to be all round him. He darted into the shadows of some dark undergrowth and crouched down behind the trunk of a tall and lumpy tree.

The halitoad came closer. Its rasping breath grew louder. Twig's palms were wet and his mouth was dry; he couldn't swallow. The fromps and the quarms fell silent, and in the awful stillness Twig's heart beat like a drum. Surely the halitoad must be able to hear it. Perhaps it had gone. Twig peered cautiously round the trunk of the tree.

MISTAKE! his brain screamed, as he found himself staring into two yellow slit-eyes glinting back at him from the darkness. A long coiled tongue flicked in and out, tasting the air. Suddenly, the halitoad inflated like a bullfrog. It was about to blast its jet of venomous breath. Twig closed his eyes, held his nose and clamped his mouth shut. He heard a fizzing hiss.

The next moment, there was a muffled thud from behind him as something fell to the ground. Twig nervously opened one eye and inspected. A fromp was lying on the forest floor. Its furry, prehensile tail was twitching. Twig remained perfectly still as the halitoad shot out its sticky tongue, grasped the hapless fromp and scuttled off with it into the under-growth.

'That was close!' Twig said, and sighed with relief. He wiped the sweat from his brow. '*Too* close!'

The moon had turned milky, and the shadows had deepened. As Twig wandered miserably on, the gloom clung to him like a damp blanket. The halitoad might be gone but that was the least of his worries. The fact remained that he had strayed from the path. Now, he was lost.

Often Twig stumbled, sometimes he fell. His hair became wet with sweat, though his bones were chilled to the marrow. He didn't know where he was going, he didn't know where he'd been; he hoped he wasn't simply going round in circles. He was also tired, yet each time he paused to rest a growl or snarl or a ferocious roar would set him trotting off again.

At last, unable to go any farther, Twig stopped. He sank to his knees and lifted his head to the sky.

'Oh, Gloamglozer!' he cursed. 'Gloamglozer! Gloam-glozer!' His voice rang out in the frosty night air. 'Please. Please. Please,' he cried. 'Let me find the path again. If only I hadn't left the path! Help me! Help me! Help . . .'

'HELP!'

The cry of distress cut through the air like a knife. Twig jumped to his feet and looked round.

'HELP ME!' It wasn't an echo.

The voice was coming from Twig's left. Instinctively, he ran to see what he could do. The next moment he stopped again. What if it was a trap? He remembered Tuntum's bloodcurdling tales of woodtrolls who had been lured to their death by the false calls of the dagger-slash, a monstrous creature with forty razor-sharp claws. It looked like a fallen log – until you stepped on it. Then its paws would snap shut, and so they would remain until the body of the victim had started to decay. For the daggerslash ate only carrion.

'For pity's sake, help me, someone,' came the voice again, but weaker now.

Twig could not ignore the desperate plea a moment longer. He drew his knife – just in case – and set off towards the voice. He hadn't gone more than twenty paces when he tripped over something sticking out from the bottom of a humming combbush.

'Ouch!' cried the voice.

Twig spun round. He'd tripped on a pair of legs. Their owner sat up and glared at him angrily.

'You oaf!' he exclaimed.

'I'm sorry, I . . .' Twig began.

'And don't stare,' he interrupted. 'It's very rude.'

'I'm sorry, I . . .' Twig said again. It was true; he *was* staring. A shaft of moonlight was shining down through the forest onto a boy, and the sight of his red-raw face, crimson hair waxed into flame-like points, and necklaces of animal teeth, had startled Twig. 'You're a slaughterer, aren't you?' he said.

With their bloodied appearance, the slaughterers looked – and sounded – ferocious. It was said that the generations of spilt blood had seeped through their pores and down into the follicles of their hair. Yet, although their business was indeed the butchery of the tilder they hunted and the hammelhorns they reared, the slaughterers were a peaceable folk.

Nevertheless, Twig could not hide his revulsion. Apart from the occasional Deepwood traveller, the slaughterers were the woodtrolls' nearest neighbours. They traded together – carved wooden items and basketware, for meat and leather goods. However, the woodtrolls, like everyone else in the Deepwoods, despised the slaughterers. They were, as Spelda put it, the bottom of the pot. No-one wanted to associate with the folk who had blood, not only on their hands, but all over their bodies.

'Well?' said Twig. 'Are you a slaughterer?'

'What if I am?' said the boy defensively.

'Nothing, I . . .' Lost in the Deepwoods, you couldn't afford to be too choosy about your companions. 'I'm Twig,' he said.

The boy touched his forehead lightly and nodded. 'My name's Gristle,' he said. 'Please take me back to my village. I can't walk. Look,' he said, and pointed to his right foot.

Twig saw the six or seven angry purple marks at the back of his heel. Already the whole foot had swollen to twice its normal size. Even as Twig watched, the swelling spread up his leg.

'What's happening?' gasped Twig.

'It's . . . it's . . .'

Twig realized the boy was staring at something behind him. He heard something hiss, and spun round. And there, hovering just above the ground, was the vilest creature Twig had ever seen.

It was long and lumpy, with luminous slime-green skin that glistened moistly in the milky moonlight. Along the length of its body were bulging yellow spots that oozed a clear liquid. Wriggling and squirming, the creature fixed Twig with its huge cold eyes.

'What is it?'
he whispered
to Gristle.

'A hover worm,' came the reply. 'Whatever you do, don't let it get you.'

'No chance,' said Twig bravely, and reached for his knife. It wasn't there. 'My knife,' he cried. 'My naming knife. I . . .' And then Twig remembered. He had been carrying it when he tripped over Gristle's legs. It must be on the ground somewhere.

Twig stared ahead, too terrified to take his eyes off the hover worm for so much as a second. The creature continued to writhe. The hissing sound was coming not from its mouth, but from rows of ducts along its underbelly. These expelled the air which kept the worm hovering aloft.

It moved nearer, and Twig found himself staring at the creature's mouth. It had rubbery lips and floppy feelers, and gulped constantly at the air. Suddenly the lips parted.

Twig gasped. The hover worm's mouth was full of tentacles, each one with a dripping sucker at the end. As the jaws widened, the tentacles sprang out and wriggled like maggots.

'The knife,' Twig muttered to Gristle. 'Find my knife.'

He heard Gristle rummaging through the dry leaves. 'I'm trying,' he said. 'I can't . . . Yes,' he cried. 'I've got it!'

'Quick!' said Twig desperately. The hover worm was quivering, ready to attack. He reached behind his back for the knife. 'Hurry UP!'

'Here!' said Gristle, and Twig felt the familiar bone handle in his palm. He closed his hand around it, and gritted his teeth.

The hover worm swayed in the air, backwards and forwards, and trembling all the while. Twig waited. Then suddenly, and with no warning, the hover worm struck. It flew at Twig's neck, mouth agape and tentacles taut. It stank of rancid grease.

Terrified, Twig leapt back. The hover worm abruptly switched direction in mid-air and came at him from the other side. Twig ducked.

The creature shot over his head, hissed to a halt, coiled itself round, and attacked again.

This time it came from the front – just as Twig had hoped. As the creature's tentacles were about to suction themselves onto his exposed neck, Twig twisted round and lunged forwards. The knife plunged into the soft underbelly of the worm, and ripped along the row of air ducts.

The effect was instant. Like a balloon that has been inflated and released, the creature spun wildly through the air with a loud *thpthpthpthppppp*. Then it exploded, and a mass of small, slimy scraps of yellow and green skin fluttered down to the ground.

'YEAH!' Twig roared and punched the air. 'I've actually been and gone and done it! The hover worm is dead.'

As he spoke, dragon's smoke billowed from his mouth. The night had become bitter with an icy north wind. Yet Twig was not cold. Far from it. A glow of pride and excitement warmed his whole body.

'Hel' me,' came a voice from behind him. It sounded strange – as though Gristle was talking while eating.

'It's OK,' said Twig as he pulled himself to his feet. I . . . GRISTLE!' he screamed.

The slaughterer was all but unrecognizable. Before

Twig's battle with the hover worm, Gristle's leg had been swollen. Now his entire body had swelled up. He looked like a huge dark red ball.

'Ta' me home,' he mumbled unhappily.

'But I don't know where your home is,' said Twig.

'I'll ta' you,' said Gristle. 'Lif' me u'. I'll give you birectio's.'

Twig bent down and gathered the slaughterer up in his arms. He was surprisingly light.

Twig started walking. 'Le',' said Gristle a while later, followed by, 'Le' agai'. Ri'. Strai' o'.' As Gristle continued to swell, even the simplest words became impossible. In the end, he had to press his podgy hands against Twig's shoulders to indicate which way to go.

If Twig had been going in circles before, he certainly wasn't now. He was being steered towards somewhere new.

'WOBBLOB!' Gristle shouted. 'BLOBBERWOBBER!'

'What?' said Twig sharply. But, even as he spoke, he realized what was happening. Gristle's body, which had been light when he'd picked it up, was now *less* than weightless. The massive, bulging mass was on the point of floating up and away.

He tried his best to hold on round Gristle's waist – at least, the place where his waist had once been – but it was impossible. It was like holding a sackful of water; the difference being that this particular sack was trying to fall *upwards*. If he let go, Gristle would disappear into the sky.

Twig wiped the sweat from his brow. Then he wedged the inflated boy between two branches, taking care to choose a tree without thorns. He didn't want Gristle to burst. He pulled the rope Spelda had given him from his shoulder, tied one end to Gristle's leg, and the other round his own waist – and set off once more.

It wasn't long before Twig was in difficulty again. With each step, the upward pull grew stronger. It became more and more difficult to remain on the ground. He clutched hold of the branches of bushes he passed, to keep himself anchored. But it was no good. The slaughterer was simply too buoyant.

All at once, Twig's legs were dragged off the ground,

his hands lost their grip on the branches, and he and Gristle floated up into the air.

Up and up, they went, into the icy night and towards open sky. Twig tore in vain at the knotted rope around his waist. It wouldn't budge. He stared down at the fast receding ground and, as he did so, something occurred to him – something awful.

Gristle would be missed. His family and friends would come looking for him when he didn't return. Twig, on the other hand, had done what woodtrolls never did. He had strayed from the path. No-one would come looking for him.

CHAPTER THREE

THE SLAUGHTERERS

As Twig continued to rise up through the cold, dark air, the rope dug painfully into the bottom of his ribs. He gasped for breath and, as he did so, a curious whiff of acrid smoke filled his head. It was a mixture of wood smoke, leather and a pungent smell that Twig couldn't identify. Above him, Gristle grunted urgently.

'Are we near your village?' Twig asked.

Gristle grunted again, more insistently this time. Suddenly, between the leaves, Twig caught sight of flickering flames and blood-red smoke. There was a fire, not twenty paces away.

'Help!' Twig bellowed. 'HELP US!'

Almost at once, the ground below him was swarming with the blood-red slaughterers, each carrying a flaming torch.

'UP HERE!' Twig shrieked.

The slaughterers raised their heads. One of them pointed. Then, without a word being spoken, they slipped into action. Calm and methodical, they removed ropes which had been hanging round their shoulders, and made slipknots at one end. Then, with the same unhurried sense of purpose, they began tossing the makeshift lassos up into the air.

Twig moaned as the ropes tumbled back through the air beneath him. He spread his legs wide and held his feet out, hooked and rigid. The slaughterers tried again, but with Gristle pulling him still higher, their task was getting more difficult by the second.

'Come on,' Twig muttered impatiently, as the slaughterers tried again and again to lasso one of his feet. Above him, he heard muffled cries as Gristle's inflated body crashed through the uppermost branches. The next instant, Twig's own head plunged into the dense green canopy. The bruised leaves gave off a lush earthy smell.

What will it look like? Twig found himself wondering. *Above* the Deepwoods. In the realm of the sky pirates.

Before he had a chance to find out, he felt something land on his hooked foot and tighten around his ankle. One of the slaughterers' ropes had found its target at last. There was a strong tug on his leg, then another and another. The leaves slapped back into his face, and the earthy smell grew stronger.

All at once, he saw the ground way down below him – and his foot with the loop of rope around his ankle. Twenty or so of the slaughterers had a hold of the other end. Slowly, jerkily, they were pulling the rope in.

When Twig's feet finally touched the ground, the slaughterers immediately turned their attention to Gristle. Working in utter silence, they slipped their ropes around his arms and legs, and took the strain. Then, one of them pulled out his knife and sliced through the rope which was still tied round Twig's chest. And Twig was free. He bent double and breathed in deeply, gratefully.

'Thank you,' he wheezed. 'I don't think I could have lasted much longer. I . . .' He looked up. With the immense bulk of Gristle tethered above them, the whole group of slaughterers was trotting back to the village. Twig had been left on his own. What was more, it was beginning to snow.

'Thanks a lot,' he snorted.

'They're worried, is all,' came a voice from behind him. Twig looked round. A slaughterer girl was standing there, her face lit up by the flickering light of her flaming torch. She touched her forehead, and smiled. Twig smiled back.

'I'm Sinew,' she said. 'Gristle's my brother. He's been missing for three nights.'

'Do you think he'll be all right?' asked Twig.

'As long as they get an antidote inside him before he explodes,' she said.

'Explodes!' cried Twig, trying not to imagine what would have happened if they *had* soared up into the sky.

Sinew nodded. 'The venom turns to hot air. And there's only so much hot air a person can take,' she added grimly. Behind her, came the sound of a gong being banged. 'Come,' she said. 'You look hungry. Lunch is about to be served.'

'Lunch?' said Twig. 'But it's the middle of the night.'

'Of course,' said Sinew, puzzled. 'I suppose you eat lunch in the middle of the *day*,' she said, and laughed.

'Well, yes,' said Twig. 'Actually, we do.'

Sinew shook her head. 'You're strange!' she said.

'No,' Twig chuckled as he followed her through the trees. 'I'm Twig!'

As the village opened up in front of him, Twig stopped and stared. It was all so very different from his own village. The slaughterers lived in squat huts, rather than tree cabins. And whereas the woodtroll cabins were all tiled with lufwood for buoyancy, the slaughterers had constructed their huts with dense leadwood which anchored them firmly to the ground. There were no doors to their dwellings, only thick hammelhornskin curtains, designed to keep out draughts, not neighbours.

Sinew led Twig towards the fire he had first glimpsed through the overhead branches. It was huge and hot, burning on a raised circular stone platform in the very centre of the village. Twig looked behind him in amazement. Although, beyond the village, the snow was falling thicker than ever, none fell inside. The dome of warmth from the blazing fire was so intense that it melted the snow away to nothing before it could ever land.

Four long trestle tables, set for lunch, formed a square around the fire. 'Sit anywhere,' said Sinew, as she plonked herself down.

Twig sat beside her and stared ahead at the roaring flames. Although the fire was burning fiercely, each and every log remained on the ground.

'What are you thinking?' he heard Sinew say.

Twig sighed. 'Where I come from,' he said, 'we burn buoyant wood – lufwood, lullabee, you know. It's all right, but you have to use a stove. I've . . . I've never seen a fire outside like this.'

Sinew looked concerned. 'Would you rather go in?'

'No!' said Twig. 'That's not what I meant. This is nice. At home – well, where I was brought up – everyone disappears inside their cabins when it's cold. It can be very lonely when the weather's bad.' Twig didn't add that it was pretty lonely for him the rest of the time, too.

By now all the benches were full and, at the far end, the first course was already being served. As a delicious fragrance wafted across, Twig realized just how hungry he was.

'I recognize that smell,' he said. 'What is it?'

'Tilder sausage soup, I think,' said Sinew.

Twig smiled to himself. Of course. The soup was a delicacy the grown-up woodtrolls got to eat on Wodgiss Night. Every year he'd wondered what it tasted like. Now he was about to find out.

'Move your elbow, love,' came a voice from behind him. Twig looked round. An old woman was standing there with a ladle in her right hand, and a round pot in her left. When she saw Twig, she drew back sharply, her smile disappeared and she gave a little shriek. 'A ghost!' she gasped.

'It's all right, Gram-Tatum,' said Sinew, leaning over. 'This is Twig. He's from Outside. It's him we have to thank for saving Gristle's life.'

The old woman stared at Twig. 'It was *you* who brought Gristle back to us?' she said.

Twig nodded. The old woman touched her forehead and bowed. 'Welcome,' she said. Then she lifted both her arms high in the air and beat the soup-pot loudly with the ladle. 'Hush up!' she cried. She climbed onto the bench and looked at the square of expectant faces. 'We have in our midst a brave young man by the name of Twig. He rescued our Gristle and brought him back to us. I want you all to raise your glasses and bid him welcome.'

All round the table, the slaughterers – young and old – stood up, touched their foreheads, raised their glasses and cried out, 'Welcome, Twig!'

Twig looked down shyly. 'It was nothing,' he mumbled.

'And now,' said Gram-Tatum, climbing back down. 'I dare say you're feeling hungry. Tuck in, love,' she said, as she ladled the soup into his bowl. 'And let's see if we can't get some colour into those cheeks of yours,' she added.

The tilder sausage soup tasted as delicious as it had smelled. Simmered until the sausages were soft, in stock seasoned with nibblick and orangegrass, the soup was rich and spicy. It was also just the start. Juicy hammel-horn steaks, rolled in seasoned knotroot flour and deep-fried in tilder oil came next, accompanied by earth-apples and a tangy blue salad. And this was followed by honey trifle and dellberry blancmange and small wafer biscuits drenched in treacle. Twig had never eaten so well – nor drunk so much. A large jug full of woodapple cider stood in the centre of each of the four tables, and Twig's mug was never allowed to empty.

As the meal went on, the atmosphere grew increas-ingly rowdy. The slaughterers forgot about their guest, and the air – already warmed by the blazing fire – became warmer still, with laughter and joking, with the telling of tales and sudden bursts of song. And when Gristle himself appeared, apparently none the worse for his ordeal, everyone went mad!

They cheered, they clapped, they whooped and whistled, their crimson faces aglow in the bright firelight. Three men jumped up and hoisted Gristle onto their shoulders, and while they paraded him round and round, the rest of the slaughterers beat their mugs on the table and sang a simple song in their deep and syrupy voices.

> 'Welcome back lost slaughterer
> Welcome like a stranger
> Welcome back from the deep deep woods
> Welcome back from danger.'

Over and over they repeated the verse – not all together, but as a round, with each table of slaughterers waiting their turn to start singing. The air was filled with swirling harmonies, more beautiful than Twig had ever heard. Unable to resist, he joined in. He banged the table to the beat with his own mug, and was soon singing the words with the rest.

After the third circuit of the tables, the men approached Twig himself. They stopped directly behind him, and placed Gristle down on the ground. Twig stood up and looked at the slaughterer boy. Everyone fell silent. Then, without saying a word, Gristle touched his forehead, stepped solemnly forwards and touched Twig on *his* forehead. His face broke into a smile. 'We are brothers now.'

Brothers! Twig thought. If only. 'Thank you, Gristle, but . . . Whoooah!' he cried, as he himself was hoisted up onto the men's shoulders.

Swaying precariously from side to side, Twig smiled, then grinned, and then laughed with delight as the men carried him once, twice, three and four times round the table, faster and faster. He looked down dizzily at the red blur of happy faces beaming back at him, and knew that he had never felt as welcome as he did now, here in the bubble of warmth and friendliness that was the slaughterers' Deepwoods home. It would be nice, he thought, if I could stay here.

At that moment, the air resounded with the sound of the gong clanging for a second time. The three slaughterers stopped running abruptly, and Twig felt the earth once again beneath his feet.

'Lunch is over,' Sinew explained as the slaughterers all jumped up from their benches and, still laughing and singing, returned to work. 'Would you like to look round?' she asked.

Twig stifled a yawn and smiled sheepishly. 'I'm not used to being up at this time,' he said.

'But it's the middle of the night,' said Gristle. 'You can't be sleepy!'

Twig smiled. 'I was up all day,' he said.

Sinew turned to her brother. 'If Twig wants to go to bed . . .'

'No, no,' said Twig firmly. 'I'd like to look round.'

They took him first to the hammelhorn pens. Twig stood on the bottom rail and looked at the shaggy beasts with their curling horns and sad eyes. They were chewing drowsily. Twig leaned over and patted one of the animals on the neck. Irritated, the hammelhorn knocked his hand away with a toss of its horned head. Twig drew back nervously.

'They may look docile,' said Sinew, 'but hammelhorns are unpredict-able animals by nature. You can't turn your back on them for a minute. Those horns can hurt!'

'*And* they're clumsy,' Gristle added. 'That's why we all have to wear thick boots.'

'We've a saying,' said Sinew. '"The smile of the hammelhorn is like the wind" – you never know when it's going to change.'

'But they do taste good!' said Gristle.

At the smoke house, Twig saw row upon row of tilder carcasses hanging on hooks. A large kiln, fuelled with redoak chips, produced a deep crimson smoke which gave the tilder ham its distinctive flavour. It was this smoke, rather than blood, which had stained the slaughterers' skin.

Not a single part of the tilder was wasted. The bones were dried and used like wood; the fat was used for cooking, for oil-lamps and candles, and for greasing the cogs of the tarp rollers; the coarse fur was spun into rope, and the antlers were carved into all kinds of objects – from cutlery to cupboard handles. It was the leather, however, which was the most valuable part of the animal.

'This is where the hide is rilked,' said Gristle.

Twig watched the red-faced men and women pummelling the hides with large round stones. 'I've heard this sound before,' he said. 'When the wind is from the north-west.'

'It softens the leather,' Sinew explained. 'Makes it easier to mould.'

'And these,' said Gristle, moving on, 'are the tanning vats. We use only the finest leadwood bark,' he added proudly.

Twig sniffed at the steaming vats. It was the smell he'd noticed when he was floating above the village.

'That's why our leather's so popular,' said Sinew.

'The best in the Deepwoods,' said Gristle. 'Even the sky pirates use it.'

Twig spun round. 'You deal with the sky pirates?' he said.

'Our best customers,' said Gristle. 'They don't come often, but when they do visit they take whatever we've got.'

Twig nodded, but his mind was elsewhere. Once again, he saw himself standing at the prow of a pirate ship, with the moon above and the wind in his hair, sailing across the sky.

'Will they be back soon?' he asked at last.

'The sky pirates?' said Gristle, and shook his head. 'It's not long since they were last here. They won't be back for a while now.'

Twig sighed. He suddenly felt immensely weary. Sinew noticed his eye-lids growing heavy. She took him by the arm.

'Come,' she said. 'You must rest. Ma-Tatum will know where you're to sleep.'

This time, Twig did not argue. Almost dead on his feet, he followed Sinew and Gristle to their hut. Inside, a woman was mixing something red in a bowl. She looked up. 'Twig!' she said, and wiped her hands on her apron. 'I've been wanting to see you.' She bustled her way towards him and enfolded him in her stubby arms. The top of her head pressed against Twig's chin.

'Thank you, Pale One,' she sobbed. 'Thank you so much.' Then she pulled herself away and dabbed at her eyes with the corner of her apron. 'Take no notice,' she sniffed. 'I'm just a silly old woman . . .'

'Ma-Tatum,' said Sinew. 'Twig needs to sleep.'

'I can see that,' she said. 'I've already put some extra bedding in the hammock. But before that, there are one or two important things I . . .' She began rummaging furiously through a chest of drawers, and the air was soon filled with the things she was *not* looking for. 'Ah, here we are!' she exclaimed at last, and handed Twig a large furry waistcoat. 'Try it on,' she said.

Twig slipped the waistcoat over his leather jacket. It fitted perfectly. 'It's so warm,' he said.

'It's a hammelhornskin waistcoat,' she told him, as she did up the toggles at the front. 'Our special- ity,' she added, 'and not for sale.' She cleared her throat. 'Twig,' she said. 'I would like you to accept it as a token of my gratitude for bringing Gristle back to me, safe and sound.'

Twig was overwhelmed. 'Thank you,' he said. 'I . . .'

'Stroke it,' said Gristle.

'What?' said Twig.

'Stroke it,' he repeated, and giggled excitedly.

Twig ran his palm down over the fleecy fur. It was soft and thick. 'Very nice,' he said.

'Now the other way,' Gristle persisted.

Twig did as he was told. This time the fur bristled and stiffened. 'YOW!' he cried, and Gristle and Sinew burst out laughing. Even Ma-Tatum was smiling. 'It's like needles,' said Twig, sucking at his hand.

'Dead or alive, you should never rub a hammelhorn up the wrong way,' Ma-Tatum chuckled. 'I'm glad you like my gift,' she added. 'May it serve you well.'

'It's very kind of you . . .' Twig began. But Ma-Tatum was not yet done.

'And this will protect you from the unseen dangers,' she said, and slipped a tooled leather charm around his neck.

Twig smirked. Mothers, it seemed, were superstitious, wherever they lived.

'You would do well not to mock,' said Ma-Tatum sharply. 'I see from your eyes that you have far to go. There is much out there that would do you harm. And though there is an antidote for every poison,' she added, and smiled at Gristle, 'once you fall into the clutches of the gloamglozer, then you're done for.'

'The gloamglozer?' said Twig. 'I know about the gloamglozer.'

'The most evil creature of all,' said Ma-Tatum, her voice cracked and low. 'It lurks in shadows. It stalks us slaughterers, sizing up its victim all the while, planning its death. Then it pounces.'

Twig chewed nervously at the end of his scarf. It was the same gloamglozer who was feared by woodtrolls – that monstrous beast which lured woodtrolls who strayed from the path to certain death. But that was just in stories, wasn't it? Even so, as Ma-Tatum continued talking, Twig shuddered.

'The gloamglozer consumes its victim while its heart is still beating,' Ma-Tatum whispered, her voice trailing away to nothing. 'RIGHT!' she announced loudly, and clapped her hands together.

Twig, Sinew and Gristle all jumped.

'Ma-aa!' Sinew complained.

'Well!' said Ma-Tatum sternly. 'You young people. Always scoffing and mocking.'

'I didn't mean . . .' Twig began, but Ma-Tatum silenced him with a wave of her blood-red hand.

'*Never* take the Deepwoods lightly,' she warned him. 'You won't last five minutes if you do.' Then she leaned forwards and seized his hand warmly. 'Now go and rest,' she said.

Twig didn't need telling twice. He followed Gristle and Sinew out of the hut, and went with them across the village square to the communal hammocks. Strung between the trunks of a triangle of dead trees, the hammocks swung gently to and fro, all the way up. Twig was, by now, so tired he could scarcely keep his eyes open. He followed Gristle up a ladder which was lashed to the side of one of the trees.

'This is ours,' said the slaughterer when they reached the uppermost hammock. 'And there's your bedding.'

Twig nodded. 'Thanks,' he said. The quilt Ma-Tatum had left for him was near the far end. Twig wobbled across the hammock on his hands and knees, and wrapped it around him. The next moment he was fast asleep.

Twig was not disturbed by the rising sun, nor by the sound of the stone slab being dragged across the ground until the fire was directly beneath the hammocks. And when it was time for Gristle and Sinew and the others of the Tatum family to go to bed, Twig didn't notice a thing as they climbed into the massive hammock and settled down all round him.

Twig slipped into a red dream. He was dancing with red people in a huge red hall. The food was red, the drink was red – even the sun streaming in through the far windows was red. It was a happy dream. A warm dream. Until the whispering began, that is.

'Very cosy, very nice,' it hissed. 'But this is not where you belong, is it?'

In his dream, Twig looked round. A gaunt, cloaked figure was slinking off behind a pillar. As it did so, it scratched a long sharp fingernail over the red surface. Twig stepped tentatively forwards. He stared at the scratch in the wood: it was weeping like an open wound. Suddenly the whispering returned directly in his ear.

'I'm still here,' it said. 'I'm *always* here.'

Twig spun round. He saw no-one.

'You silly little fool,' came the voice again. 'If you want to discover your destiny, you must follow *me*.'

Twig stared in horror as a bony hand with yellow talons emerged from the folds of the cloak, reached up and clasped the hood. It was about to reveal its face. Twig tried to turn away, but he couldn't move.

All at once, the creature cackled with hideous laughter and let its hand drop down by its side. 'You shall know me soon enough,' it hissed, and leaned towards him conspiratorially.

Twig's heart pounded furiously. He felt the warmth of the creature's breath against his ear, and smelt a sulphurous mustiness which seeped from its hooded cloak.

'WAKE UP!'

The sudden cry exploded inside Twig's head. He shouted out in fear, opened his eyes and looked around him in confusion. It was light and he was high up, lying on something soft. Beside him were red-skinned individuals, all snoring softly. He looked at Gristle's face, calm in sleep and everything came back to him.

'Wakey WAKEY, up there,' he heard.

Twig clambered to his knees and looked over the edge of the hammock. Far below him was a slaughterer – the only one still up. He was stoking the fire.

'Was that you?' Twig called down.

The slaughterer touched his forehead lightly and nodded. 'Ma-Tatum told me not to let you sleep through the day, Master Twig,' he called back. 'Not with your being a creature of the sun.'

Twig looked up at the sky. The sun was almost at its highest. He made his way to the end of the hammock, taking care not to wake any of the slumbering family, and climbed down the ladder.

'That's it, Master Twig,' said the slaughterer, and helped him down from the bottom rung. 'You've a long journey in front of you.'

Twig frowned. 'But I thought I might stay awhile,' he said. 'I like it here and I won't be missed by Cousin Snetterbark – at least, not for the time being . . .'

'Stay here?' said the slaughterer in a sneering voice. 'Stay here? Oh, you wouldn't fit in here at all. Why, Ma-Tatum said only this daybreak what a gawky, ugly little fellow you are, with no feeling for leather . . .'

'Ma-Tatum said that?' Twig swallowed the lump rising in his throat. 'But she gave me this coat,' he said, touching it lightly. The fur bristled and stood on end. 'Ouch!' he yelped.

'Oh, that,' wheedled the slaughterer. 'You don't want to take no notice of that. It's just an old coat. Can't give them away normally,' he added, and laughed spitefully. 'No. You want to go back to your own kind, and the path you want lies just over that way.'

The slaughterer pointed into the forest. As he did so a flock of grey birds billowed noisily up into the sky.

'I will!' said Twig. His eyes were smarting but he wouldn't cry – not in front of this little man with his red face and fiery hair.

'And watch out for the gloamglozer!' the slaughterer called out, his voice nasal and mocking, as Twig reached the trees.

'I'll watch out for the gloamglozer, all right,' muttered Twig. 'And for stuck-up slaughterers who treat you like a hero one minute and a barkslug the next!'

He turned to say as much, but the slaughterer was already gone. Twig was on his own once more.

.CHAPTER FOUR.

THE SKULLPELT

As the forest, green, shadowy and forbidding, closed in around him once more Twig nervously fingered the talismans and amulets round his neck, one by one. If there was some powerful evil at the heart of the Deepwoods, then could these small pieces of wood and leather truly be enough to keep it at bay?

'I hope I'll never have to find out,' he muttered.

On and on Twig walked. The trees became unfamiliar. Some had spikes, some had suckers, some had eyes. All of them looked dangerous to Twig. Sometimes they grew so close together that, despite his misgivings, Twig had no choice but to squeeze between their gnarled trunks.

Time and again, Twig cursed his shape and size. Unlike the woodtrolls and slaughterers, who were short, or the banderbear, which was strong, he was not designed for a life in the Deepwoods.

And yet, when the trees abruptly thinned out, Twig grew still more anxious. There was no sign of the promised path. He glanced over his shoulder for any creature that might mean him harm as he scurried across the wide dappled clearing as quickly as he could, and back into the trees. Apart from a small furry creature with scaly ears which spat at him as he passed, none of the Deepwoods inhabitants seemed interested in the gangly youth hurrying through their domain.

'Surely if I keep going, I'll reach the path,' he said. 'Surely!' he repeated, and was shocked by how small and uncertain his voice sounded.

Behind him an unfamiliar high-pitched squeal echoed round the air. It was answered by a second squeal to his left, and a third to his right.

I don't know what *they* are, thought Twig. But I don't like the sound of them.

He kept walking straight ahead, but quicker now. Beads of sweat broke out across his forehead. He bit into his lower lip and started to run. 'Go away,' he whispered. 'Leave me alone.'

As if in response, the squeals echoed louder and closer than before. Head lowered and arms raised, Twig ran faster. He crashed through the undergrowth. Creepers lashed his body. Thorns scratched his face and hands. Branches swung across his path, as if trying to trip him up or knock him senseless. And all the while the forest was growing deeper and denser and – as the canopy of leaves closed above his head – dismally dark.

Suddenly, Twig found himself staring at a turquoise

light which sparkled like a jewel far away in front of him. For a moment he wondered whether the unusual colour might signal danger. But only for a moment. Already, the strains of soft hypnotic music were washing over him.

As he got closer, the light spilled out onto the leafy forest floor. Twig looked down at his feet, awash with turquoise-green. The music – a swirl of voices and strings – grew louder.

Twig paused. What should he do? He was too frightened to go on. But he couldn't go back. He *had* to go on.

Chewing on the edge of his scarf, Twig took a step forwards. Then another. And another ... The turquoise light washed all over him, so dazzling he had to shield his eyes. The music, loud and sad, filled his ears. Slowly, he lowered his hands and looked around.

Twig was standing in a clearing. Although the turquoise light was bright, it was also misty. Nothing was clear. Shadowy shapes floated before his eyes, crossed one another, and disappeared. The music grew louder still. All at once, a figure stepped out of the mist and stood before him.

It was a woman, short and stocky, with beaded tufts of hair. Twig couldn't see her face.

'Who are you?' he asked. And yet, as the music rose to a slushy crescendo, Twig knew the answer to his question. The short stumpy legs, the powerful shoulders and, when she moved her head to one side, the profile of that rubbery nose. Apart from the strange clothes she was wearing, there was no doubt.

'Mother-Mine,' said Twig softly.

But Spelda turned away, and began to walk off into the turquoise mist. The unfamiliar blue fur gown she was wearing trailed along the ground behind her.

'DON'T GO!' Twig bellowed after her. 'MOTHER! SPELDA!'

The music grew increasingly frantic. The singing voices became discordant.

'COME BACK!' Twig cried, and he sprinted off after her. 'DON'T LEAVE ME!'

He ran and ran through the dazzling mist. Sometimes he knocked into branches and stumps he hadn't seen, sometimes he tripped and fell sprawling to the ground. Each time, he picked himself up, brushed himself down and set off once more.

Spelda had come looking for him; that much was clear. She must have known I was in trouble, he thought; that I strayed from the path. She's come to take me home after all. I can't lose her now!

Then Twig saw her again. She was standing some way ahead, with her back to him. The music had become soft and gentle, and the voices sang a soothing lullaby. Twig approached the figure, his whole body tingling with expectation. He ran up to her, calling out her name. But Spelda didn't move.

'Mother,' Twig cried. 'It's me.'

Spelda nodded and turned slowly. Twig was shaking from head to toe. Why was she acting so strangely?

The music was low. Spelda was standing in front of Twig, head bowed, and with the hood of the fur gown hanging down over her face. Slowly, she opened her arms to him, to wrap him up in her warm embrace. Twig stepped forwards.

At that moment, Spelda let out a terrible scream and staggered back, flapping wildly at her head. The music became loud again. It beat, urgent and rhythmical, like a pounding heart. She screamed a second time – a savage cry that chilled Twig to the bone – and struck out frantically at the air around her.

'Mother-Mine!' Twig cried. 'What's happening?'

He saw blood trickling down from a gash on her scalp. Another cut appeared on her shoulder, and yet another on her back. The blue gown turned to violet as the blood spread. And still she writhed and screamed and lashed out at her unseen assailant.

Twig stared aghast. He would have helped if he could. But there was nothing – absolutely nothing at all – that he could do. He had never felt so useless in his life.

Suddenly, he saw Spelda clutching at her neck. Blood gushed out between her fingers. She whimpered softly, collapsed, and lay on the ground twitching horribly.

Then she fell still.

'NOOOOO!' Twig wailed. He dropped to his knees and shook the body by the shoulders. There was no sign of life. 'She's dead,' he sobbed. 'And it's all my fault. Why?' he howled. 'Why? Why? Why?'

Burning tears ran down his face and splashed onto the bloodstained gown as Twig hugged his mother's lifeless body.

'That's it,' came a voice from above his head. 'Let it all out. Wash the lies away.'

Twig looked up. 'Who's there?' he said, and wiped his eyes. He saw nothing, no-one. The tears continued to come.

'It's me, and I'm here,' said the voice.

Twig stared up at the place the voice was coming from, but still couldn't see anything. He jumped to his feet. 'Come on, then!' he screamed, and pulled the knife from his belt. 'Try having a go at me!' He stabbed at the air wildly. 'COME ON!' he roared. 'SHOW YOURSELF, YOU COWARD!'

But it was no good. The invisible assassin remained invisible. Revenge would have to wait. Tears of sorrow, of frustration, of rage streamed down Twig's cheeks. He couldn't stop.

Then something strange began to happen. At first Twig thought he was imagining it. But no. Everything around him was slowly changing. The mist thinned, the turquoise light began to dim – even the music faded away. Twig discovered he was still in the forest after all. More alarmingly, as he looked round, he saw what it was that had spoken to him.

'You!' Twig gasped. He recognized the creature from the tales that Taghair had told him. It was a caterbird, or rather *the* caterbird, for each of their number considered themselves to be one and the same. The pain of loss rose in his throat. 'Why did you do it?' he blurted out. 'Why did you kill Spelda? My own mother!'

The great caterbird cocked its head to one side. A shaft of sunlight glinted off the massive horned bill, and a purple eye swivelled round to inspect the boy.

'It wasn't your mother, Twig,' it said.

'But I saw her,' said Twig. 'I heard her voice. She *said* she was my mother. Why would she . . .'

'Take a look,' it said.

'I . . .'

'Look at her fingers. Look at her toes. Pull back her hair and look at her face,' the caterbird insisted. 'Then tell me it's your mother.'

Twig returned to the body and crouched down. Already, it looked different. The coat now looked less like an item of clothing, more like real fur. He ran his gaze along the outstretched arm, and realized that no sleeve could ever be so tight fitting. He moved around the body, and suddenly caught sight of a hand: three scaly fingers tipped with orange claws. And the feet were the same. Twig gasped and looked back at the caterbird. 'But . . .'

'The face,' the bird said firmly. 'Look at the face, and see what I saved you from.'

With trembling fingers, Twig reached forwards and pulled back the crumpled fur. He yelped with horror. Nothing could have prepared him for what he saw.

Taut scaly skin, like brown oilpaper wrapped around a skull; bulging yellow eyes, glaring blindly back at him; and the mouth with its rows of hooked teeth, contorted by rage and pain.

'What is it?' he asked quietly. 'The gloamglozer?'

'Oh, no, not the gloamglozer,' replied the bird. 'There are some who call it a skullpelt,' it said. 'A hunter of dreamers who lose their way in the lullabee groves.'

Twig looked up. There were lullabee trees all around, humming softly in the dappled light. He touched the scarf round his neck.

'When among the lullabee trees,' the bird went on, 'you see only what the trees want you to see – until it is too late. It was lucky for you that I hatched when I did.'

Above the caterbird a giant cocoon dangled like a discarded sock.

'You hatched from that?' said Twig.

'Naturally,' said the caterbird. 'Where else? Aah, little one, you have so much to learn. Taghair was right.'

'You know Taghair?' Twig gasped. 'But I don't understand.'

The caterbird tutted impatiently. 'Taghair sleeps in our cocoons and dreams our dreams,' it explained. 'Yes, I know Taghair, as I know all other caterbirds. We share the same dreams.'

'I wish Taghair was here now,' said Twig sadly. 'He'd know what I ought to do.' His head was throbbing from the hum of the trees. 'I'm useless,' he sighed. 'A miserable excuse for a woodtroll. I strayed from the path. I'm lost for ever and I've nobody to blame but myself. I wish that . . . that the skullpelt had torn me limb from limb. At least that would have been an end to it!'

'Now, now,' said the caterbird gently, and hopped down beside him. 'You know what Taghair would say, don't you?'

'I don't know *anything*,' Twig wailed. 'I'm a failure.'

'He would say,' the caterbird went on, 'if you stray from the well-trodden path, then tread your own path for others to follow. Your destiny lies beyond the Deepwoods.'

'*Beyond* the Deepwoods?' Twig looked up into the caterbird's purple eyes. 'But there is no beyond to the Deepwoods. The Deepwoods go on for ever and ever. There is up and there is down. The sky is up and the woods are down, and that is that. Every woodtroll knows that this is so.'

'Every woodtroll sticks to the path,' said the caterbird softly. 'Maybe there is no *beyond* for a woodtroll. But there is for you.'

Suddenly, with a loud clap of its jet-black wings, the caterbird leaped from the branch and soared up into the air.

'STOP!' Twig yelled. But it was already too late. The great caterbird was flapping away over the trees. Twig stared miserably ahead of him. He wanted to shout, he wanted to scream, but the fear of attracting the attention of one of the fiercer Deepwoods' creatures kept his mouth clamped firmly shut.

'You were at my hatching and I shall watch over you always,' came the caterbird's distant call. 'When you truly need me, I shall be there.'

'I truly need you now,' Twig muttered sulkily.

He kicked the dead skullpelt. It gave a long, low groan. Or was it just the sound of the lullabee trees? Twig didn't wait to find out. He left the lullabee grove and ran headlong off into the endless, pathless depths of the dark and sombre Deepwoods.

The forest was dark with night once more when Twig stopped running. He stood, hands on hips and head bowed, gasping for breath. 'I ca . . . can't go another st . . . step,' he panted. 'I just can't.'

There was nothing else for it. Twig would have to find a safe place to spend the night. The tree nearest to him had a massive trunk and a thick covering of broad green leaves which would protect him if the weather worsened. More importantly, it looked harmless. Twig collected together a pile of dry fallen leaves and pushed them into a dip between the roots of the tree. Then he crawled onto his makeshift mattress in his makeshift cot, curled himself into a ball and closed his eyes.

All around him the night sounds whined, wailed and screamed. Twig folded his arm over his head to cut out the unnerving din. 'You'll be all right,' he said to himself. 'The caterbird promised to watch over you.'

And with that he drifted off to sleep, unaware that at that moment, the caterbird was otherwise engaged with a family of bushnymphs, many many miles away.

CHAPTER FIVE

THE BLOODOAK

At first it was just a tickle, which Twig swatted away in his sleep. He smacked his lips drowsily and rolled over onto his side. Nestling in his cot of leaves beneath the ancient spreading tree, Twig looked so young and small and vulnerable.

A long, thin squirmy creature it was doing the tickling. As Twig's breathing grew more regular once again, it wriggled around in mid-air directly in front of his face. It flexed and writhed in the warm air each time Twig breathed out. All at once, it darted forwards and began probing the skin around the boy's mouth.

Twig grumbled sleepily, and his hand brushed at his lips. The squirmy creature dodged the slender fingers, and scurried up into the dark tunnel of warmth above.

Twig sat bolt upright, instantly wide awake. His heart pounded. There was something up his left nostril!

He grabbed his nose and squeezed it till his eyes watered. Abruptly, the whatever-it-was scraped down over the soft membrane inside his nose, and was out. Twig winced, and his eyes screwed shut with pain. His heart pounded all the more furiously. What was there? What could it possibly be? Fear and hunger wrestled with one another in the pit of Twig's stomach.

Scarcely daring to look, Twig peered out through the crack in one eye. Catching sight of a flash of emerald-green, Twig feared the worst, and scuttled back on his hands and feet. The next moment, he slipped, his legs shot out in front of him and he came crashing down on his elbows. He stared back into the gloomy half-light of the new morning. The wriggly green creature had not moved.

'I'm being silly,' Twig muttered. 'It's just a caterpillar.'

Leaning back, he squinted up into the dark canopy. Behind black leaves, the sky had turned from brown to red. The air was warm, but the backs of his legs were damp with the early morning moisture of the Deepwoods. It was time to make a move.

Twig climbed to his feet and was brushing the twigs and leaves out of the hammelhornskin waistcoat when – WHOOOOSH – the air hissed with a sound like a lashing whip. Twig gasped, and stared in frozen horror as the emerald green caterpillar lunged at him and flew round his outstretched wrist once, twice, three times.

'Aaaargh!' he screamed as sharp thorns dug into his skin – and he cursed himself for letting his guard slip.

For the wriggly green creature wasn't a caterpillar at all. It was a creeper, a tendril, the emerald tip of a long and viciously barbed vine that writhed and swayed through the shadowy forest like a serpent, seeking out warm-blooded prey. Twig had been lassoed by the terrible tarry vine.

'Let me go!' he cried, tugging frantically at the stout vine. 'LET ME GO!'

As he pulled, so the claw-like thorns punctured his skin and sank deep into the softness of his inner arm. Twig yelped with pain and watched, terrified, as tiny crimson beads of blood grew and burst and trickled down over his hand.

A thick, sickly wind stirred his hair and ruffled the fur of his hammelhornskin waistcoat. It carried the scent of his blood into the shadows. From out of the darkness came the soft clattering noise of a thousand razor-sharp

83

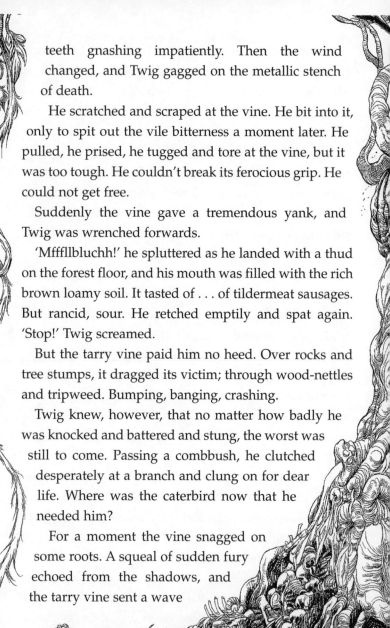

teeth gnashing impatiently. Then the wind changed, and Twig gagged on the metallic stench of death.

He scratched and scraped at the vine. He bit into it, only to spit out the vile bitterness a moment later. He pulled, he prised, he tugged and tore at the vine, but it was too tough. He couldn't break its ferocious grip. He could not get free.

Suddenly the vine gave a tremendous yank, and Twig was wrenched forwards.

'Mfffllbluchh!' he spluttered as he landed with a thud on the forest floor, and his mouth was filled with the rich brown loamy soil. It tasted of . . . of tildermeat sausages. But rancid, sour. He retched emptily and spat again. 'Stop!' Twig screamed.

But the tarry vine paid him no heed. Over rocks and tree stumps, it dragged its victim; through wood-nettles and tripweed. Bumping, banging, crashing.

Twig knew, however, that no matter how badly he was knocked and battered and stung, the worst was still to come. Passing a combbush, he clutched desperately at a branch and clung on for dear life. Where was the caterbird now that he needed him?

For a moment the vine snagged on some roots. A squeal of sudden fury echoed from the shadows, and the tarry vine sent a wave

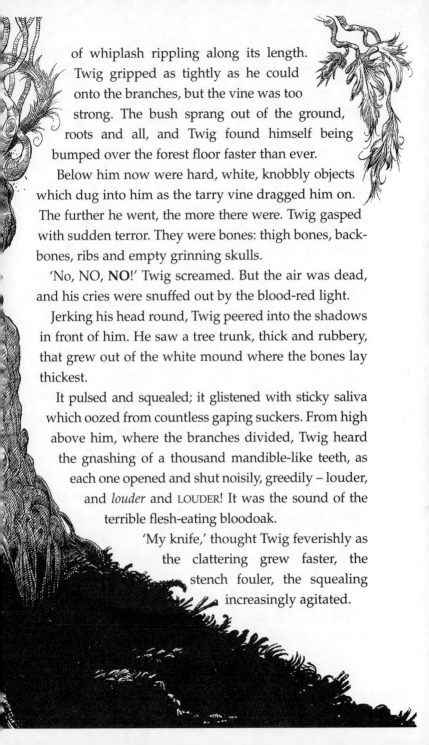

of whiplash rippling along its length. Twig gripped as tightly as he could onto the branches, but the vine was too strong. The bush sprang out of the ground, roots and all, and Twig found himself being bumped over the forest floor faster than ever.

Below him now were hard, white, knobbly objects which dug into him as the tarry vine dragged him on. The further he went, the more there were. Twig gasped with sudden terror. They were bones: thigh bones, backbones, ribs and empty grinning skulls.

'No, NO, **NO**!' Twig screamed. But the air was dead, and his cries were snuffed out by the blood-red light.

Jerking his head round, Twig peered into the shadows in front of him. He saw a tree trunk, thick and rubbery, that grew out of the white mound where the bones lay thickest.

It pulsed and squealed; it glistened with sticky saliva which oozed from countless gaping suckers. From high above him, where the branches divided, Twig heard the gnashing of a thousand mandible-like teeth, as each one opened and shut noisily, greedily – louder, and *louder* and LOUDER! It was the sound of the terrible flesh-eating bloodoak.

'My knife,' thought Twig feverishly as the clattering grew faster, the stench fouler, the squealing increasingly agitated.

He fumbled around on his belt feverishly and gripped the smooth handle of his naming knife. Then, with one swift movement, he pulled it from its sheath, swung his arm over his head and brought the blade down with all his strength.

There was a sound of soggy splintering, and a spurt of glistening green slime squirted into his face. Yet, as his arm suddenly jerked back, Twig knew he'd done it. He wiped the slime from his eyes.

Yes! There it was, the vine, swaying hypnotically to and fro above him. Back and forwards it went, back and forwards, to and fro. Twig was rooted to the spot. He watched, transfixed, as the severed end stopped dripping and the liquid congealed to form a knobbly green blob at the end of the vine, the size of his fist.

Abruptly, the rubbery skin split, the blob burst open and, with a rasping slurp, a long tentacle tipped with emerald-green sprang out. It sensed the air and quivered.

Then a second tentacle appeared, and a third. Twig stared, unable to move. Where one vine had been, now there were three. They reared up, ready to strike and – S-S-S-SWOOOOOSH – all three of them lunged.

Twig screamed with pain and terror as the tentacles lashed themselves tightly round his ankles. Then, before he could do anything about it, the tarry vine tugged his feet out from under him and hoisted him, upside down, high up into the air.

The whole forest blurred before Twig's eyes as the blood rushed to his head. It was all he could do to keep hold of the knife. Wriggling and squirming and grunting with effort, he heaved himself up, clung hold of the vine, and began jabbing and stabbing.

'FOR SKY'S SAKE, LET ME GO!' he cried.

Green slime immediately began bubbling to the surface. It oozed round the knife and over his hand, oily and slippery. Twig lost his grasp and tumbled back through the air.

Dangling helplessly by his feet, he twisted his neck back and looked down. He was above the top of the main tree-trunk. Directly beneath him were the thousand razor-sharp teeth he had heard clattering so greedily. Arranged in a wide circle, they glinted in the red light.

All at once, they sprang open. Twig found himself staring down into the crimson gorge of the bloodthirsty tree. It slobbered and slavered noisily. The stench was atrocious. Twig gagged emptily.

Now he would never ride the sky pirates' ships. Nor reach his destiny. Nor even leave the Deepwoods.

With his last bit of strength, Twig struggled frantically to pull himself upwards again. The hammelhornskin waistcoat slipped down over his eyes. He felt the fur stiffen as he rubbed it the wrong way. Again and again, he reached up and – finally – he managed to clutch hold of the vine. As he did so, it released his feet.

Twig cried out with fear as he swung loose, and dug in with his fingernails. Now, instead of trying to cut himself free, he was desperate to hold on – desperate not to be dropped down into the gaping mouth of the bloodoak. Hand over hand, he tried to climb the vine but, slippery with the slime, it slid back between his fingers. For every inch he went up, he slithered back half a dozen.

'Help,' he whimpered softly. 'Help me.'

The vine gave a violent jerk. Twig lost his grip and the tarry vine flicked him away.

Feet first, arms flailing, he dropped through the air. He landed with a sickening squelch deep down inside the cavernous mouth of the flesh-eating bloodoak. The teeth snapped shut above his head.

It was pitch black in the tree, and loud with the sound of hideous gurgling. 'I can't move,' he gasped. All round him, the monstrous throat constricted, and rings of hard woody muscle squeezed him tightly. 'Can't bre . . . e . . . eathe!'

One thought went round and round his head, too awful to take in. *I'm being eaten alive!* Deeper and deeper down he went. *Eaten alive . . .'*

Suddenly the bloodoak juddered. A rumbling, grumbling burp burbled up from the inner depths of the tree, and a blast of foul air rushed up past Twig. For an instant, the muscles released their grip.

Twig gasped and slipped down a little further. The thick hair on the hammelhornskin waistcoat bristled as it was brushed up the wrong way. The bloodoak juddered again.

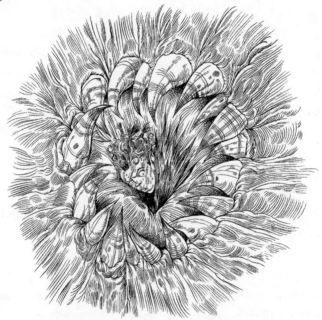

The gurgling grew louder as the bloodoak continued to cough, until the whole spongy tube shook with a deafening roar. Beneath him, Twig felt something strange pressing against the bottom of his feet, pushing him upwards.

All at once, the retching tree released its grip on Twig's body for a second time. It had to get rid of the spiky object which had become lodged in its throat. It burped, and the pressure of air which had built up below suddenly exploded with such violence that it shot Twig back up the hollow trunk.

He burst into the air with a loud *POP* and soared off in a shower of spittle and slime. And for a moment, Twig felt he was actually flying. Up and away he went, as free as a bird.

And then down again, crashing through branches, as he hurtled back to the ground. He landed with a heavy thud that jarred every bone in his body. For a moment he lay there, scarcely daring to believe what had happened.

'You saved my life,' he said, smoothing the fur of the hammelhornskin waistcoat. 'Thank you for your gift, Ma-Tatum.'

Hurt, but not that badly, it occurred to Twig that something must have broken his fall. He reached below him tentatively.

'Oy!' a voice protested.

Startled, Twig rolled over and looked up. Not some*thing*, but some*body*! He tightened his grip on the knife, still in his hand.

CHAPTER SIX

THE GYLE GOBLIN COLONY

Twig climbed shakily to his feet, and looked at the character lying on the ground. He had a flat head, a bulbous nose and heavy-lidded eyes; he was dressed in filthy rags and covered in dirt from head to toe. He stared at Twig suspiciously.

'You did drop down on us from a great height,' he said.

'I know, I'm sorry about that,' said Twig, and shuddered. 'You wouldn't believe what I've just been through. I . . .'

'You did hurt us,' the goblin interrupted. His nasal voice buzzed round inside Twig's head. 'Are you the gloamglozer?' it said.

'The gloamglozer?' said Twig. 'Of course not!'

'The most terrifying creature in all the Deepwoods, it be,' the goblin said, its ears twitching. 'It does lurk in the dark corners of the sky and drop down upon the unsuspecting.' The goblin's eyes became two thin slits. 'But then perhaps you do know that already.'

'I'm no gloamglozer,' Twig said. He returned his knife to its sheath, reached forwards and helped the goblin to his feet. The bony hand felt hot and sticky to the touch. 'I'll tell you what, though,' Twig added. 'I was almost *eaten* just now – by a bloodo . . .'

But the goblin was no longer listening. 'He does say he is not the gloamglozer,' he called into the shadows.

Two more of the squat, angular goblins appeared. Apart from the differing patterns of streaked dirt on their faces, the three of them were identical. Twig's nose wrinkled up at the sickly sweet odour they gave off.

'In that case,' said the first, 'we do best return to the colony. Our Grossmother will wonder where we are.'

The others nodded, picked up their bundles of weeds and swung them up onto their flat heads.

'Wait!' Twig cried. 'You can't just go. You've got to help me. COME BACK!' he yelled, and sped off after them.

The forest was dense and overgrown. Through cracks in the canopy, Twig saw that the sky had turned to pinky-blue. Little light penetrated the gloom beneath.

'Why won't you listen to me?' said Twig miserably.

'Why should we?' came the reply.

Twig trembled with loneliness. 'I'm tired and hungry,' he said.

'So what!' they jeered.

Twig bit into his lower lip. 'And I'm lost!' he shouted angrily. 'Can't I go with you?'

The goblin directly in front of him turned and shrugged. 'It be all the same to us what you do.'

Twig sighed. It was the nearest to an invitation he was likely to get. At least they hadn't said he *couldn't* go with them. The goblins were unpleasant but, as Twig had already learned, you couldn't afford to be too fussy in the Deepwoods. And so, picking out the tarry vine's thorny splinters from his wrist as he went, Twig did go with them.

'Do you have names?' he called out, some while later.

'We are gyle goblins,' they all replied as one.

A little farther after that, they were suddenly joined by three more goblins, and then another three – and then half a dozen more. They all looked the same. It was only the objects balanced on their flat heads that singled them out. One was carrying a wicker tray of berries, one, a basket of knotted roots, another, a huge bulbous gourd of purple and yellow.

All at once, the thronging crowd emerged from the forest and Twig was swept along with them into a sunlit clearing. In front of him stood a magnificent construction made of a pink, waxen material, with sagging windows and drooping towers. It was as tall as the tallest trees and stretched back farther than Twig could see.

The goblins began chattering excitedly. 'We are back,' they cried, as they surged forwards. 'We are home. Our

Grossmother will be pleased with us. Our Grossmother will feed us.'

Squeezed on all sides by the crush of bodies, Twig could hardly breathe. Suddenly, his feet left the ground and he found himself being carried on against his will. A great gateway loomed up in front of him. The next moment he was sucked beneath the towering arch in the flood of gyle goblins, and on into the colony itself.

Once inside, the goblins hurried off in all directions. Twig tumbled to the floor with a thud. More and more of the goblins continued to pour in. They stepped on his hands, they tripped over his legs. With one arm raised protectively, Twig struggled to his feet and tried in vain to get back to the door.

Jostled and bounced, he was driven across the hall and down one of the many tunnels. The air became closer, clammier. The walls were sticky and warm and glowed with a deep pink light.

'You've got to help me,' Twig pleaded as the goblins shoved past him. 'I'm hungry!' he cried, and grabbed a long woodsap from one of the passing baskets.

The goblin, whose fruit it was, turned on him angrily. 'That does not be for you,' he snapped, and snatched the woodsap back.

'But I *need* it,' said Twig weakly.

The goblin turned his back, and was gone. Twig felt anger bubbling up inside him. He was hungry. The goblins had food – yet they wouldn't let him have any. All at once his anger exploded.

The goblin with the woodsaps hadn't got far. Barging

past the others, Twig steadied himself, threw himself at the goblin's ankles – and missed.

He sat up, dazed. He was lying next to a narrow alcove set back in the wall. It was into this opening that the goblin had darted. Twig smiled grimly as he climbed to his feet. He had the goblin cornered.

'You!' he yelled. 'I want some of that fruit and I want it now.'

The red woodsaps gleamed in the pink light. Twig could already taste their syrupy flesh on his tongue.

'I did tell you once,' said the goblin as he swung the basket down off his head. 'They do not be for you.' And with that, he tipped the entire load of woodsaps down a hole in the floor. Twig heard them bouncing down a long chute and landing far below – with a muffled *plattsh*.

Twig stared at the goblin open-mouthed. 'Why did you do *that*?' he said.

But the goblin left without saying a word.

Twig slumped to the floor. 'Horrible little beast,' he muttered. Others came with their loads of roots, fruits, berries and leaves. None of them noticed Twig. None of them heard him pleading for something to eat. Eventually, Twig fell silent and stared down at the sticky floor. The stream of goblins dwindled.

It was only when a latecomer arrived, grumbling to himself about the time, that Twig looked up again. The goblin looked flustered. His hands shook as he tipped his load of succulent yellow tubroots down the hole.

'At last,' he sighed. 'Now for some food.'

Food. *Food*! The wonderful word echoed round Twig's

head. He leapt up and followed the goblin.

Two right turns and a left fork later, Twig found himself in a vast, cavernous chamber. It was round and high and domed, with glistening walls and thick pillars like dripping candles. The air was cloying with the familiar sickly sweet smell, and sticky on the skin.

Although packed, the chamber was quite still. The gyle goblins were all staring upwards, open-mouthed and wide-eyed, at a point in the very centre of the domed ceiling. Twig followed their gaze and saw a wide tube slowly descending. Clouds of pink steam billowed out from its end, making the stuffy air more stifling still.

The tube came to a halt inches above a trough. The goblins held their breath as one. There was a click and a gurgle, a final puff of steam, and all at once a torrent of thick, pink honey poured out of the bottom of the tube and into the trough.

At the sight of the honey, the goblins went wild. Voices were raised, fists flew. Those at the back surged forwards, while those at the front fought with each other. They scratched, they scraped, they tore at one another's clothes in a frenzied effort to be first at the steaming pink honey.

Twig drew back, away from the rioting goblins. He felt behind him for the wall and worked his way around the outside of the chamber. And when he came to a flight of stairs, he climbed it. Halfway to the top, he stopped, sat, and looked down on the goblins.

The pink honey was splashing and splattering everywhere as the goblins struggled to get as much of the

gooey mixture as they could. Some were slurping from
their cupped hands. Some had plunged their heads into
the sticky mess and were gulping it down in greedy
mouthfuls. One had jumped into the trough and was
lying directly under the tube with his mouth open. A
look of mindless contentment spread over his spattered
features.

Twig shook his head in disgust.

All at once, there was a loud CLONK and the stream of
pink honey stopped. Feeding time was over. A half-
hearted groan went up and several of the goblins
clambered into the trough to lick it clean. The rest began
to file away; calmly, peacefully. Along with their hunger,
the frantic atmosphere had also disappeared.

The chamber was all but empty when Twig climbed to his feet. He paused. There was another noise. PUFF-PANT, it went. SQUELCH, CLATTER. And again. PUFF-PANT, SQUELCH, CLATTER.

Heart pounding, Twig spun round and peered up into the darkness above him. He fingered his amulets nervously.

PUFF-PANT, SQUELCH, CLATTER.

Twig gasped with terror. Something was approaching. Something he didn't like the sound of one tiny little bit.

PUFF-PANT, SQUELCH, CLATTER, G-R-O-A-N!

All at once, the doorway at the top of the stairs was filled with the BIGGEST, the FATTEST, the MOST MONSTROUSLY OBESE creature Twig had ever *ever* EVER seen. She – for it was female – moved her head and surveyed the scene below her. Beady eyes peered over her fat cheeks, and the rolls of blubber around her neck wobbled.

'No peace for the wicked,' she muttered. Her voice sounded like bubbling mud. Plob plob plob plob plob. 'Still,' she added softly, shifting the mop and bucket in her hands. 'Grossmother's boys be worth it.'

She squished and squeezed herself through the doorway, wodge by wobbling wodge. Twig leaped to his feet, flew down the stairs and hid in the only place there was to hide – beneath the trough. The noise continued – PUFF-PANT, SQUELCH, CLATTER. THUD! Twig peeked nervously out.

The Grossmother was moving quickly for one so immense. Closer she came, closer and closer. Twig shivered with dread, 'She must have seen me,' he groaned, and shrank back as far into the shadows as he could.

The bucket clattered to the floor, the mop plunged into the water and the Grossmother began cleaning the mess her 'boys' had left. In the trough and around it she slopped, humming wheezily as she worked. Finally, she seized the bucket and threw the remaining water *underneath* the trough.

Twig yelped with surprise. The water was icy cold.

'What was that?' the Grossmother shrieked, and began prodding and jabbing beneath the trough with her mop. Time and again, Twig dodged out of the way. But then his luck ran out. The mop slammed into his chest and sent him skidding backwards, out into the open. The Grossmother was upon him at once.

'Ugh!' she exclaimed. 'Vile . . . disgusting . . . revolting VERMIN! Contaminating my beautiful colony.'

She seized Twig by the ear, swung him up off the ground and plonked him into the bucket. Then she rammed the mop down on top of him, picked the whole lot up and hauled herself back to the top of the stairs.

Twig lay still. His chest ached, his ear throbbed – the bucket swayed. He heard the Grossmother squeeze herself back through the door, and then through another. The sweet, sickly smell grew stronger than ever. Suddenly the swaying stopped. Twig waited a moment, then pushed the mop aside and peered over the edge.

The bucket was hanging from a hook, high up above a vast steamy kitchen. Twig gasped. There was no way down.

He watched the Grossmother wobble across the room to where two massive pots were bubbling away on a stove. She seized a wooden paddle and plunged it into the simmering pink honey. 'Stir, stir, stir,' she sang. 'Got to keep it stirring.'

Then she dipped a podgy finger into the pot, and sucked it thoughtfully. Her face broke into a smile. 'Perfect,' she said. 'Though perhaps we could do with just a little more.'

She laid the paddle down and heaved her massive bulk over to a shadowy recess at the back of the kitchen. There, looking out of place next to the cupboards and table, Twig saw a well. The Grossmother seized the wooden handle and began turning. When the end of the rope suddenly popped up into view, she looked perplexed.

'Where's the blooming bucket got to?' she muttered.

Then she remembered.

'Unnh!' she grunted with surprise a moment later, as she unhooked the bucket and glanced inside. 'I did forget to put the rubbish out.'

Twig stared out of the bucket nervously as the Grossmother lumbered back to the sink. What exactly did 'putting the rubbish out' involve? He discovered all too soon as a powerful jet of water – so cold it took his breath away – thundered down onto him. He felt himself spinning round and round as the Grossmother swilled the bucket.

'Whooaaah!' he cried out dizzily.

The next moment, the Grossmother tipped the bucket up and sloshed the whole lot – Twig and all – down the disposal chute.

'Aaaarrgh!' he screamed as he tumbled, over and over, helter-skelter all the way down to the bottom of the long chute, out and – *PLATTSH* – onto a warm, soft, soggy mound.

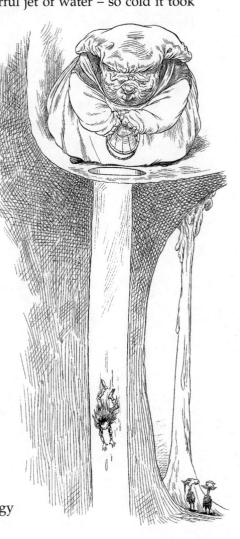

Twig sat up and looked round. The long, flexible tube he'd fallen down was only one of many. All of them were swaying gently this way and that, illuminated by the roof of waxy pink which glowed far, far above his head. He would never be able to climb back up that high. What was he to do now?

'First things first,' Twig thought, his eye catching sight of a woodsap, still intact, lying on the rotting pile to his right. He picked it up and wiped it on his hammelhorn-skin waistcoat till the red skin gleamed. He bit into the fruit hungrily. Red juice dribbled down his chin.

Twig smiled happily. 'Scrumptious!' he slurped.

.CHAPTER SEVEN.

Spindlebugs and Milchgrubs

Twig finished the woodsap and tossed the core away. The painful gnawing in his stomach had gone. He climbed to his feet, wiped his hands on his jacket and looked round. He was standing at the centre of a huge compost heap in an underground cavern as colossal as the colony above it.

Gritting his teeth and trying hard not to breathe in, Twig squelched across to the far side of the rotting vegetation and climbed up onto the enclosing bank. He stared up at the ceiling far above his head. 'If there's a way in,' he muttered grimly, 'there *must* be a way out.'

'Not necessarily,' came a voice.

Twig started. Who had spoken? It was only when the creature moved towards him, and the light glinted on its translucent body and wedge-shaped head, that Twig realized how close it was.

Tall and angular, it looked like some kind of giant glass insect. Twig had never seen anything like it before. He knew nothing of the underground swarms of spindlebugs, nor of the lumbering milchgrubs they tended.

Suddenly, the insect lunged forwards and seized Twig's collar in its claws. Twig cried out as he found himself face to face with the twitching head, all waving feelers and huge multi-faceted eyes, which gleamed green and orange in the dim light.

'I got another one over here,' the creature called. There was the sound of approaching scurrying, and the spindlebug was joined by three others.

'I don't know what's the matter with her upstairs,' said the first.

'Downright sloppy, I call it,' said the second.

'She'd be the first one to complain if the honey was off,' said the third. 'We'll *have* to have a word with her.'

'Fat lot of good that'll do,' said the first. 'If I've told her once, I've told her a thousand times . . .'

'VEGETABLE, NOT ANIMAL!' they all cried together, and trilled with irritation.

The insect holding Twig stared at him closely. 'Not like the usual pests we get,' it observed. 'This one's got hair.' Then, without any warning, it lurched to one side and bit savagely into Twig's arm.

'YOUCH!' Twig screamed.

'Eeeeyuk!' squealed the spindlebug. 'It's *sour!*'

'What did you do that for?' Twig demanded.

'*And* it can talk!' said another in surprise. 'You'd best get it into the incinerator before it can cause any trouble.'

Twig gasped. The *incinerator*? He wrenched himself free of the insect's pincer-grip, and dashed off along the criss-cross of raised walkways. A shrill buzz of alarm immediately went up as the four furious insects gave chase.

As Twig ran, so the underground landscape began to change. He passed field after field being hoed and raked by more of the gardening insects. Further on, and the soil was dotted with the pink spots of something beginning to sprout. Further still, and the fields were full of glistening pink fungus that grew up like spongy antlers.

'Now we've got you,' came a voice.

Twig skidded to a halt. Two of the spindlebugs were in front of him. He turned. The other two were advancing from behind. There was nothing else for it. Twig leapt

down from the walkway and raced across the field, crushing a swathe through the pink fungus as he ran.

'HE'S IN THE FUNGUS BEDS,' the insects screeched. 'HE MUST BE STOPPED!'

Twig's heart sank when he realized he was not the only one amongst the pink toadstools. The whole field was full of huge, lumbering creatures, as transparent as the insects, and all busy grazing on the fungus.

Twig saw the chewed food coursing through tubes inside the bodies, down into the stomach, and along the tail to a huge, bulbous sac filled with a pink liquid. One of the beasts glanced up and let out a low growl. Others joined in. Before long the air was throbbing with the sound of roaring.

'DETAIN THE PEST!' came the shrill cry of the gardener

insects. The milchgrubs began to advance.

Twig darted this way, that way, dodging between the massive animals as they blundered towards him. Slipping and sliding on the crushed fungus, he made it to the far side only just in time. Even as he was scrambling up the bank, he felt the warm breath of one of the milchgrubs, as the beast snapped at his ankles.

Twig looked around him anxiously. To his left and right was the walkway, but both directions were blocked. Behind him were the milchgrubs, trundling ever closer. In front was a grooved slope which disappeared down into the shadows.

'Now what?' he panted. There was no choice. He *had* to go down the slope. He spun round and hurtled headlong into the shadowy darkness.

'NOW HE'S HEADING FOR THE HONEY PIT!' the spindlebugs screeched. 'CUT HIM OFF. *NOW*!'

But with their massive honey sacs which they dragged carefully behind them, the milchgrubs were slow. Twig soon left them far behind as he raced down the slope. If I can just . . . Twig thought. Suddenly the ground opened up before him. Twig cried out. He was running too fast to stop.

'NO!' His legs pedalled desperately in mid-air. 'AAAARGH!' he screamed, and plummeted down.

PLOP!

He landed in the middle of a deep pool and sank. A moment later, he resurfaced, coughing and spluttering, and splashed about frantically.

The clear pink liquid was warm and sweet. It filled Twig's ears and eyes, his mouth; some of it slipped down his throat.

He stared up at the sheer sides of the pit and groaned. Things had gone from bad to worse. He'd *never* be able to climb out.

Far above him the spindlebugs and milchgrubs were coming to the same conclusion. 'Nothing to be done,' Twig heard them saying. '*She'll* have to sort it out. *We've* got work to do.'

And with that – as Twig struggled to tread water in the sticky liquid – the spindlebugs crouched down and began tugging at teats on the milchgrubs' honey sacs. Pink jets squirted down into the pit.

'They're milking them,' Twig gasped in amazement. The sticky pink honey landed all round him. 'GET ME OUT!' he roared. 'You *can't* leave me here . . . blobber blobber blob blob . . .'

Twig had begun to sink. The hammelhornskin waistcoat which before had saved his life, now threatened to take it. Its thick fleece had soaked up the sticky liquid and become heavy. Down, down, down Twig was dragged, eyes open, down into the viscous pinkness. He tried to swim back to the surface, but his arms and legs had turned to wood. He was at the end of his strength.

Drowndead in rosy honey, he thought miserably.

And as if *that* wasn't bad enough, he realized that he wasn't alone. Something was disturbing the calmness of the pool. It was a long snake-like creature with a massive head which was thrashing through the pink liquid. Twig's heart pounded in his ears. Drowndead or devoured. What a choice! He squirmed round and kicked out wildly.

But the beast was too quick for him. Its body snaked round behind him, and the wide gaping jaws came up from underneath – and swallowed him whole.

Up, up, up, he rose, through the rosy syrup and . . . out. Twig gasped and coughed and gulped down huge lungfuls of air. He wiped his eyes clean and, for the first time, saw the long body and massive head for what they really were. A rope and a bucket.

Past the steep walls he went; past the group of angular spindlebugs, still busy squeezing the last drops of pink honey from the now deflated sacs of their milchgrubs, and on into the upper reaches of the great cavern. The bucket swung perilously. Twig clung onto the rope, scarcely daring, though unable *not*, to look down.

Far below was the patchwork of pink and brown fields. Above him, a black hole in the glowing roof was coming nearer and nearer and . . .

All at once his head popped out, and Twig found himself back in the steamy heat of the kitchen. The fat and flabby face of the Grossmother was directly in front of him.

'Oh, no,' Twig groaned.

Sweat rolled down over the Grossmother's bulging brow and cheeks as she secured the end of the rope. Her body wobbled with every movement, sloshing and slewing like a sackful of oil. Twig ducked down as she unhooked the bucket, and prayed she wouldn't notice the crown of his head above the surface of the honey.

Humming tunelessly, the Grossmother slopped the full bucket over to the stove, hefted it up onto her trembling shoulder and sloshed the contents into a pot. Twig fell into the bubbling goo with a squelchy *ploff*.

'Ugh!' Twig exclaimed, his disgust drowned out by the Grossmother's puffing and panting as she returned to the well for more. 'What's going on?'

The honey was hot – hot enough to turn the clear bucketful instantly opaque. It gurgled and plopped all round him, splashing into his face. Twig knew he had to get out before he was boiled alive. He heaved himself up out of the thickening steamy mixture onto the rim of the pot and splatted down onto the top of the stove.

Now what? he wondered. The floor was too far down to risk jumping, and the Grossmother was already returning with yet another bucket of honey from the well. He scuttled off behind the pot, crouched down and hoped she wouldn't see him.

With his heart beating fit to burst, Twig listened to the Grossmother hum and stir and sip the pink honey as it came to the boil. 'Hmmm,' she mumbled, and smacked her lips noisily. 'Tastes a bit funny,' she said thoughtfully. 'Sort of sour . . .' She sipped again, and hiccuped. 'Oh, I'm sure it's fine.'

She plodded off and snatched a couple of tea towels from the table. Twig looked round him desperately. The honey was now ready. It was time it was poured into the feeding tube. Surely she'll see me! he thought.

But Twig was in luck. As the Grossmother wrapped the cloths around the first scalding pot, and heaved it from the stove, Twig ducked round behind the second. And when she plonked it back into place and went to empty the second pot, he darted behind the first. The Grossmother, intent on getting the honey for her boys ready in time, never noticed a thing.

Twig remained hidden as the Grossmother struggled to empty the second huge pot into the feeding tube. After a considerable amount of grunting and groaning, he heard a ratchet clicking round. He peeked out.

The Grossmother was pulling a lever up and down. As she did so, the long tube, now full of the heated pink honey, sank down through the floor and into the chamber below. She pulled a second lever, and he heard the click and gurgle of the honey being released into the trough. A roar of gluttonous joy echoed up from the hall below.

'There you are,' the Grossmother whispered, and a satisfied smile spread over her gargantuan features. 'Sup well, my boys. Enjoy your meal.'

Twig scraped the sticky honey off his jacket and licked his fingers.

'Yeuch!' he said and spat out. Boiled up, the honey tasted vile. He wiped his mouth on the back of his hand. It was time for him to make his getaway. If he waited for the Grossmother to do the washing-up, he'd be caught for sure. And the last thing he wanted was to be dropped back down the disposal chute. But where *was* the Grossmother?

Twig squeezed himself between the two empty pots and peered round. He couldn't see her anywhere.

Meanwhile, the tumultuous racket from the chamber below showed no sign of easing up. If anything it was getting louder and – to Twig's ears – more agitated.

The Grossmother, too, must have sensed that something was wrong. 'What is it, my treasures?' Twig heard her saying.

He twisted round in alarm, and squinted into the shadows. And there she was, her monstrous bulk sprawled out in an armchair in the far corner of the kitchen. Her head was back and she was dabbing at her brow with a damp cloth. She looked worried.

'What *is* it?' she said a second time.

Twig didn't care what was wrong. This was his chance

to escape. If he knotted the tea towels together, he should be able to shin down to the floor. He squeezed back between the pots but too quickly. In his haste, he knocked against one of the pots and could only stare in horror as it toppled over, away from him. For an instant it hovered in mid-air, before crashing to the floor with a resounding CLANG!

'Oh, me!' the Grossmother squeaked and leaped to her feet with remarkable speed. She saw the fallen pot. She saw Twig. 'Aaaaah!' she screamed, her beady eyes blazing. 'More vermin! And at my cooking pots!'

She grabbed her mop, raised it in front of her and advanced purposefully towards the stove. Twig quaked where he stood. The Grossmother brought the mop up above her head and . . . froze. The expression on her face turned from one of fury to one of utter terror.

'You . . . you haven't been *in* the honey, have you?' she said. 'Tell me you haven't. Contaminating it, adulterating it . . . you vile and disgusting little creature. Anything can happen if the honey is soured. *Anything*. It turns my boys wild, it does. You don't know . . .'

At that moment the door behind her burst open and a furious cry of 'THERE SHE BE!' went up.

The Grossmother swung round. 'Boys, boys,' she said sweetly. 'You *know* the kitchens are out of bounds.'

'Get her!' the goblins screamed. 'She did try to poison us.'

'Of course I didn't,' the Grossmother whimpered as she backed away from the advancing torrent of goblins.

She turned, raised a flabby arm and pointed a fat finger at Twig. 'It was . . . *that*!' she squealed. 'It got into the honey pot.'

The gyle goblins were having none of it. 'Let's do her!' they raged. The next instant they were all over her. Scores of them. Screaming and shouting, they pulled her to the ground and began rolling her over and over across the sticky kitchen floor to the disposal chute.

'It was just a bad . . . *ooof* . . . a bad batch,' she grumbled. 'I'll . . . *unnh* . . . My stomach . . . ! I'll make a new lot.'

Deaf to her excuses and promises, the goblins rammed her head down the chute. Her increasingly desperate cries became muffled. The goblins leaped to their feet and jumped up and down on her massive bulk, trying to push her down through the narrow opening. They squished her. They squeezed her. They pummelled and pounded her until all at once, with a squelchy *plopff*, the immense wobbling body of fat disappeared.

Meanwhile, Twig had finally got down from the stove and made an immediate dash for it. Just as he reached the door, he heard a colossal SPLODGE! echoing up through the hole. He knew that the Grossmother had landed on one of the compost heaps in the great cavern below.

The goblins whooped and cheered with malicious delight. Their poisoner had been dealt with. But they weren't satisfied yet. They turned their anger on the kitchen itself. They smashed the sink. They trashed the stove. They snapped off the levers and broke the tube.

They sent the pots and stirring paddles tumbling down the chute, and roared with laughter when a cry of 'Ouch, my head!' came echoing up from the cavern below.

And *still* they weren't done! With a howl of fury they turned on the well, hitting it, kicking it, breaking it into a thousand little bits, till all that was left was a hole in the floor.

'Get the cupboards! Get the shelves! Get her arm-chair!' they yelled, and they pushed and shoved everything they could lay their hands on down through the hole they had made. Finally, all that was left in the kitchen was Twig himself. A bloodcurdling cry went up, like the roar of a wounded animal raging with pain. 'Get *him*!' the goblins screamed.

Twig spun round, raced through the door and dashed off down the dimly lit tunnel. The gyle goblins pounded after him.

To the left and to the right, Twig ran.

This way and that.

On and on through the
endless maze of the
honeycombed
colony.

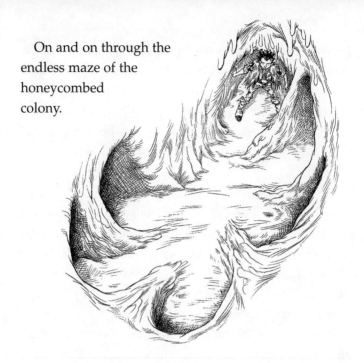

The sound of the raging goblins gradually faded away
to nothing.

'I've lost them,' said Twig with a sigh of relief. He
looked round at the tunnel, stretching away in front and
behind. He swallowed nervously. 'I've also lost *myself*,'
he muttered miserably.

Some minutes later, Twig came to a crossroads. He
stopped. His stomach churned. There were twelve
tunnels leading off it, like the spokes of a wheel.

'Which way *now*?' he said, and groaned. Everything
had gone wrong. Everything! Not only had he strayed
from the path, now he'd even managed to stray from the
forest!' And *you* wanted to ride a sky ship,' he said to
himself bitterly. 'Some chance! A stupid, gangly little

mistake for a woodtroll, that's all you are.' And in his head he heard the voices of Spelda and Tuntum chiding him once again. 'He wouldn't listen. He never learns.'

Twig closed his eyes. A lost child once more, he did what he had always done when a choice proved too big for him: he stuck his arm out and began to spin round.

> 'Which? What? Where? Who?
> I do choose YOU!'

Opening his eyes, Twig stood and stared down the tunnel which chance had selected for him.

'Chance is for the ignorant and weak,' came a voice that turned Twig's skin to gooseflesh.

He spun round. There in the shadows stood one of the goblins. His eyes glinted like fire. What was this new twist to the gyle goblin's behaviour? Twig wondered.

'If you do truly want to get out of the colony, Master Twig,' the goblin said, more softly now, 'you must follow me.' So saying, he turned on his heel and marched off.

Twig swallowed nervously. Of course he wanted to get out, but what if this was just a trick? What if he was being led into an ambush?

It was hot in the tunnel, so stiflingly hot he felt dizzy and sick. The low waxy ceiling oozed sticky drops which plashed on his head and slid down his neck. His stomach ached for something to eat.

'I've got no choice,' he whispered.

The goblin's cloak flapped round a corner and disappeared from sight. Twig followed.

The pair of them walked along tunnels, up and down flights of stairs and through long empty chambers. The air was rank with the smell of staleness and decay; it was hard to breathe and Twig's head spun. His skin was clammy; his tongue was dry.

'Where are we going?' he called out weakly. 'I reckon you're as lost as I am.'

'Trust me, Master Twig,' came the wheedling reply and, even as he spoke, Twig felt a cool draught hit his face.

He shut his eyes and breathed in the fresh air. When he opened them again, the goblin was out of sight. The next moment, as he rounded a corner, Twig saw light. Sunlight! Streaming in through the towering arched doorway.

Twig broke into a run. Faster and faster he sprinted, scarcely able to believe that he'd made it. Down the final tunnel . . . across the hall . . . and OUT!

'YES!' he shouted.

In front of him stood a group of three gyle goblins. They turned round and stared at him dully.

'All right?' said Twig cheerfully.

'Do we look all right?' said one.

'Our Grossmother did try to poison us,' said another.

'So we did punish her,' said the third.

The first one looked down at his dirty bare feet miserably. 'But we did act too hastily,' he said.

The others nodded. 'Who will feed us now? Who will protect us from the gloamglozer?' they said.

Suddenly, all three of them burst into tears. 'We *need* her,' they wailed in unison.

Twig stared back at the dirty gyle goblins in their filthy rags and snorted. 'You *need* to think for yourselves,' he said.

'But we're tired and hungry,' the goblins whined.

Twig stared back at them angrily. 'So . . .' He paused. He was about to say 'so what?', as the three unhelpful goblins had said to him before. But he was not a gyle goblin. 'So am I,' he said simply. 'So am I.'

And with that he turned away from the gyle goblin colony, crossed the courtyard and marched back into the surrounding Deepwoods.

.CHAPTER EIGHT.

THE BANDERBEAR

Twig undid the toggles of his fleecy jacket as he walked on. The wind had changed direction and there was an autumnal feel to the air. The weather was as unpredictable as everything else in the treacherous Deepwoods.

All round him, the forest was dripping as a recent fall of snow rapidly melted from the canopy above. Still hot, Twig stopped, closed his eyes and turned his face upwards. The icy water splashed onto his face. It was cool and refreshing.

Suddenly, something large and heavy struck Twig's head – BOOF – so hard that he was knocked to the ground. He lay still, not daring to look. What had hit him? The gloamglozer? Could the fearsome creature *really* exist? If it did, it was no use cowering. Twig opened his eyes, jumped to his feet and drew his knife.

'Where are you?' he screamed. 'Show yourself!'

Nothing appeared. Nothing at all. And the only sound to be heard was the steady 'drip drip drip' from the trees. Then came the second BOOF. Twig spun round. A huge pillow of snow, which must have slipped from the branches overhead, had completely flattened a combbush.

Twig put his hand up. There was snow in his hair. There was snow all around him. He started to laugh. 'Snow,' he said. 'That's all it is. Just snow.'

The dripping increased as Twig continued on his way. Like heavy rain it was, pouring down below. Twig was soon wet through and, as he trudged deeper into the Deepwoods, the ground became more and more boggy. Every step became an effort – an effort made all the worse by hunger.

'With the slaughterers,' he muttered. 'That was the last time I had a proper meal. And Sky knows how long ago that was.'

Twig looked up. The sun was bright and even down on the diamond-dappled forest floor he could feel its ripening warmth. Fragile twists of mist were coiling up from the soggy soil. And as the hammelhornskin dried out, Twig himself began to steam.

His hunger was impossible to ignore. It squirmed and gnawed inside his stomach. It growled impatiently. 'I know, I know,' said Twig. 'And as soon as I find some-thing, you can have it. The trouble is, what?'

When he came to a tree heavy with a deep, dark purple harvest, he stopped. Some of the round, plump pieces of fruit were so ripe they had split their skins and were dripping golden juice. Twig licked his lips. The fruit looked so juicily sweet, so succulently delicious. He reached up and clasped one.

It was soft to the touch and came away from its stalk with a slurp. Twig turned it over in his hand. He polished it on his furry waistcoat. Slowly, he brought it to his mouth and . . .

'No!' he said. 'I dare not.' And he hurled the fruit away. His stomach gurgled angrily. 'You'll have to wait,' Twig snapped, and marched grimly on, muttering under his breath about how stupid he'd been even to *consider* eating something unknown. For although many of the fruits and berries in the Deepwoods were sweet and nourishing, many more were deadly.

A single drop of juice from the rosy heartapple, for instance, was enough to kill you on the spot. And death was far from the only danger. There was fruit which could blind you, fruit which could explode inside you, fruit which could leave you paralysed. There was one, the scrapewort berry, which brought you out in a warty blue rash that never disappeared. And there was another, the pipsap, which shrank those who ate it – the more you ate, the smaller you became. Those unfortunates who had too many disappeared altogether.

'*Much* too dangerous,' Twig said to himself. 'I'll just have to hang on till I come to a tree I do recognize.'

Yet, as Twig continued through the Deepwoods, of all the countless different types of tree he saw, there wasn't a single one that looked familiar.

'This is what comes of growing up with woodtrolls,' he sighed wearily.

Since they never strayed from the path, the woodtrolls relied on others to provide them with fruit from the Deepwoods. They were barterers, not foragers. Now, more than ever before, Twig wished this were not the case.

Trying hard to ignore his stomach's protests, Twig tramped on. His body felt heavy but his head was oddly light. Mouth-watering fragrances wafted towards him from the fruit trees, while the fruits themselves seemed to glow enticingly. For hunger is a curious creature. It dulls the brain, but heightens the senses. And when a twig cracked, far away in front of him, Twig heard it as though it had broken right beside him.

He stopped dead and peered ahead. Someone or something was there. Twig advanced, taking care not to tread on any of the brittle twigs himself. Closer he went, darting from tree to tree. He heard something moan close by and crouched down out of sight. Then, heart chugging, he edged slowly forwards, peered nervously round – and found himself face to face with a huge and hairy mountain of a beast.

It was rubbing the side of its furry face gently with one massive clawed paw. When their eyes met, the creature threw back its head, bared its teeth and howled at the sky.

'Aaaargh!' Twig screamed, and scrambled back behind the tree. Shaking with fear, he heard the splinter and crack of snapping branches as the beast lumbered off, crashing its way through the undergrowth. All at once the noise stopped, and the air filled with a plaintive yodel. The next instant, from far away, a second voice yodelled in reply.

'Banderbears!' said Twig.

He'd heard them often enough before, but this was the first Twig had seen. It was even bigger than he'd imagined.

Although prodigiously large and strong, the banderbear is a timid creature. Its large doleful eyes are said to see the world larger than it really is.

Twig peeked round the tree again. The banderbear had gone. A trail of crushed vegetation led back into the forest. 'That's one path I *won't* be taking,' he said. 'I . . .'

He froze to the spot. The banderbear had *not* gone. It was standing there, not ten paces away. With its pale green fur, it was almost perfectly camouflaged. 'Wuh!' it groaned softly and raised a giant paw to its cheek. 'Wuu-uh?'

The creature was truly massive, at least twice as tall as Twig himself, and built like a vast pyramid. It had tree-trunk legs, and arms so long its knuckles grazed the ground. The four claws at the end of each limb were all as long as Twig's forearms, as were the two tusks that curved up from its jutting lower jaw. Only its ears – delicate winglike objects, constantly on the flutter – did not look as though they had been hewn from rock.

The banderbear fixed Twig with its sad eyes. 'Wuu-uh?' it groaned again.

It was in pain, that much was clear. Despite its size, it looked oddly vulnerable. Twig knew it must need his help. He took a step forwards. The banderbear did the same. Twig smiled. 'What's the matter?' he said.

The banderbear opened its mouth wide and prodded around clumsily inside with a single claw. 'Uh-uuh.'

Twig swallowed nervously. 'Let me see,' he said.

The banderbear came closer. It moved by placing both forepaws on the ground and swinging its hind legs forwards. As it approached, Twig was surprised to see grey-green moss growing in its fur. It was this that made the banderbear appear green.

'Wuh,' it grunted as it stopped in front of the boy. It opened its mouth and Twig was struck by a blast of putrid warm air. He winced and turned his face away. 'WUH!' the banderbear grunted impatiently.

Twig looked up. 'I . . . I can't reach that high,' he explained. 'Even on tiptoes. You'll have to lie down,' he said and pointed at the ground.

The banderbear nodded its enormous head and lay at Twig's feet. And, as Twig looked down into its huge and sorrowful eyes, he saw something unexpected quivering there in the dark green depths. It was fear.

'Open wide,' Twig said softly, and he opened his own mouth to show what he meant. The banderbear followed suit. Twig found himself staring into the creature's cavernous mouth, over the rows of savage teeth and down the gaping tunnel of its throat. Then he saw it, at

the back of the mouth on the left; a tooth so rotten it had
turned from yellow to black.

'Sky above!' Twig exclaimed. 'No wonder you're in
pain.'

'Wuh wuh, wh-uuuh!' the banderbear groaned and
tugged his hand repeatedly away from its mouth.

'You want me to pull it out?' said Twig.

The banderbear nodded, and a large tear rolled down
from the corner of each eye.

'Be brave,' Twig whispered. 'I'll try not to hurt.'

He knelt down, rolled up his sleeves and took a closer
look at the inside of the banderbear's mouth. The tooth,
though dwarfed by the two huge tusks, was still the size
of a small mustard pot. It was nestling in gum so red and
swollen, it looked ready to burst. Twig reached gingerly
in and clasped the rotten tooth.

The banderbear immediately flinched and turned sharply away. One razor-sharp tusk scraped across Twig's arm, drawing blood. 'Yow! Don't do that!' he shouted. 'If you want me to help you, you must keep perfectly still. Got that?'

'Wuh-wuh!' the banderbear mumbled.

Twig tried again. This time, although its huge eyes narrowed with pain, the banderbear did not move as Twig grasped the tooth.

'Tug and twist,' he instructed himself as he tightened his grip on the pitted tooth. He braced himself ready. 'Three. Two. One. NOW!' he yelled.

Twig tugged and twisted. He tugged so hard he toppled backwards, wrenching the tooth round as he did so. It juddered and rasped as the roots were torn from the gum. Blood and pus spurted out. Twig crashed down to the ground. In his hands was the tooth.

The banderbear leaped up, eyes flashing furiously. It bared its teeth, it beat its chest, it shattered the silence of the Deepwoods with a deafening roar. Then, overcome with a terrible rage, it began tearing wildly at the surrounding forest. Bushes were uprooted, trees knocked down.

Twig stared in horror. The pain must have driven the creature crazy. He struggled to his feet and tried to slip away before the beast could turn its fury on him . . .

But he was already too late. The banderbear had caught sight of him out of the corner of its eye. It swung round. It tossed aside an uprooted sapling. 'WUH!' it bellowed and bounded towards him, all wild eyes and glinting teeth.

'No,' Twig whispered, terrified that he was about to be torn limb from limb.

The next instant the banderbear was upon him. He felt its massive arms wrapping themselves around his body and smelled the musty odour of mossy fur as he was crushed against the creature's belly.

And there the two of them remained. Boy and banderbear, hugging each other gratefully in the dappled light of the Deepwoods afternoon.

'Wuh-wuh,' said the banderbear at last, and loosed its arms. It pointed inside its mouth and scratched its head questioningly.

'Your tooth?' said Twig. 'I've got it here,' and he held it out to the banderbear on the palm of his hand.

Delicately for one so immense, the banderbear took the tooth and wiped it on its fur. Then it held it up to the light so that Twig could see the hole which had been eaten right the way through. 'Wuh,' it said, and touched the amulets around Twig's neck. It handed the tooth back.

'You want me to wear it round my neck?' said Twig.

'Wuh,' said the banderbear. 'Wuh-wuh.'

'For good luck,' said Twig.

The banderbear nodded. And when Twig had slipped it onto the thong with Spelda's lucky charms it nodded again, satisfied.

Twig smiled. 'Feel better now?' he said.

The banderbear nodded solemnly. Then it touched its chest and extended its arm towards Twig.

'Is there something you can do for me in return?' said Twig. 'Not half! I'm starving,' he said. 'Food, food,' he added, and patted his stomach.

The banderbear looked puzzled. 'Wuh!' it grunted, and swung its arm round in a wide arc.

'But I don't know what's safe to eat,' Twig explained. 'Good? Bad?' he said, pointing to different fruits.

The banderbear beckoned, and led him across to a tall bell-shaped tree with pale green leaves and bright red fruit, so ripe it was dripping. Twig licked his lips greedily. The banderbear reached up, plucked a single piece of fruit in its claws and held it out for Twig.

'Wuh,' it grunted insistently, and patted its own stomach. The fruit was good; Twig should eat.

Twig took the fruit and bit into it. It was more than good. It was delicious! Sweet, succulent and with a hint of woodginger. When it was gone, he turned to the banderbear and patted his stomach again. 'More,' he said.

'Wuh,' grinned the banderbear.

*

They made an odd couple – the furry mountain and the stick boy – and occasionally Twig would ask himself why the banderbear stuck round. After all, it was so big and strong, and knew so much about the secrets of the Deepwoods that it didn't need Twig.

Maybe it, too, had felt lonely. Maybe it was grateful to him for pulling out the aching tooth. Or maybe it was simply that the banderbear liked him. Twig hoped so. Certainly *he* liked the banderbear – he liked him more than anyone he had ever known. More than Taghair. More than Gristle. More even than Hoddergruff, when the two had still been friends. How far away and long ago his life with the woodtrolls seemed.

Twig realized that by now cousin Snetterbark must have sent word that he hadn't arrived. What must they be thinking? He knew what Tuntum's gruff response would be. 'Strayed from the path,' he could hear his father saying. 'Always knew he would. He was never a woodtroll. His mother was too soft on him.'

Twig sighed. Poor Spelda. He could see her face, wet with tears. 'I told him,' she would weep. 'I told him to stay on the path. We loved him like one of our own.'

But Twig wasn't truly one of theirs. He didn't belong – not with the woodtrolls, nor with the slaughterers and certainly not in the sticky honeycombs of the gyle goblin colony.

Perhaps this is where he belonged, with the lonely old banderbear in the endless Deepwoods, wandering from meal to meal, sleeping in the soft, safe, secret places that only banderbears know. Always on the move, never staying in one place for long, and never following a path.

Sometimes, when the moon rose above the ironwood pines, the banderbear would stop and sniff the air, its small ears fluttering and its eyes half closed. Then it would take a deep breath and let out a forlorn yodelling call into the night air.

From far, far away, there would come a reply: another solitary banderbear calling back across the vastness of the Deepwoods. Perhaps one day they would stumble across each other. Perhaps not. That was the sorrow in their song. It was a sorrow Twig understood.

'Banderbear?' he said, one sweltering afternoon.

'Wuh?' the banderbear replied, and Twig felt a giant paw on his shoulder, powerful yet gentle.

'Why do we never meet the banderbears you call to at night?' he asked.

The banderbear shrugged. That was simply the way it was. It reached up and picked a green star-shaped fruit from a tree. It prodded it, sniffed it – and growled.

'No good?' said Twig.

The banderbear shook its head, split the fruit open with a claw and let it drop to the ground. Twig looked round.

'What about them?' he said, pointing up to a small round yellow fruit dangling far above his head.

The banderbear stretched up and pulled off a bunch. Sniffing all the while, it turned the fruit over and over in its massive paws. Then it gently removed an individual fruit from the bunch, nicked the skin with its claw and sniffed again. Finally, it touched the bead of syrup against the tip of its long black tongue and smacked its lips. 'Wuh-wuh,' it said at last, and handed the whole bunch over.

'Wonderful,' Twig slurped. How lucky he was to have the banderbear to show him what he could and couldn't eat. He pointed to himself, then to the banderbear. 'Friends,' he said.

The banderbear pointed to himself, and then to Twig. 'Wuh,' he said.

Twig smiled. High above him but low in the sky, the sun sank, and the light in the forest turned from lemon yellow to a rich golden glow, that poured through the leaves like warm syrup. He yawned. 'I'm tired,' he said.

'Wuh?' said the banderbear.

Twig pressed his hands together and rested the side of his head against them. 'Sleep,' he said.

The banderbear nodded. 'Wuh. Wuh-wuh,' it said.

As they set off, Twig smiled to himself. When they had first met, the banderbear's snoring had kept him awake. Now, he would have found it hard to fall asleep without the comforting rumble beside him.

They continued walking, with Twig following the path that the banderbear made through the dense undergrowth. Passing a spiky blue-green bush, Twig reached out absentmindedly and picked a couple of the pearly white berries that grew in clusters at the base of each spike. He popped one of them into his mouth.

'Are we nearly there?' he asked.

The banderbear turned. 'Wuh?' it said. Suddenly its wide eyes grew narrow and its wispy ears began to flap.

'WUUUH!' it roared, and made a lunge at the boy.

What was the matter now? Had the banderbear gone crazy again?

Twig turned on his heels and leaped out of the way of the massive beast as it hurtled towards him. It could crush him without even meaning to. The banderbear crashed to the ground, flattening the vegetation. 'WUH!' it roared again, and swung at him savagely.

The blow caught Twig on the arm. It sent him spinning round. His hand opened and the pearly berry flew off into the undergrowth. Twig landed on the ground with a bump. He looked up. The banderbear was towering above him menacingly. Twig went to scream. As he did so, the other berry – the one in his mouth – slid back and lodged itself in the back of his throat. And there it remained.

Twig coughed and spluttered, but the berry would not shift. His face went from pink to red to purple as he gasped for air. He staggered to his feet and stared up at the banderbear. Everything was beginning to swim in front of his eyes. 'Can' bre'!' he groaned, and clutched at his throat.

'Wuh!' the banderbear cried out. It grabbed Twig by the ankles.

Twig felt himself being hoisted upside down into the air. The banderbear's heavy paw began pummelling his back. Again and again it thumped down but *still* the berry would not budge. Again and again and . . .

POP!

The berry shot out of Twig's mouth and bounced across the ground.

Twig gasped and gulped at the air. Panting uncontrollably, he squirmed and wriggled upside down in the banderbear's grasp. 'Down,' he rasped. The banderbear scooped Twig up with its free arm and lay him gently on a pile of dry leaves. It crouched low and pushed its face up close.

'Wuh-wuh?' it said.

Twig looked into the concerned face of the banderbear. Its eyes were open wider than ever. It frowned questioningly. Twig smiled and wrapped his arms around the banderbear's neck.

'Wuh!' it said.

The banderbear pulled away and looked Twig in the eye. Then it turned and pointed at the berry that had so nearly choked him. 'Wuh-wuh,' it said angrily, clutched at its stomach and rolled on its back in mock agony.

Twig nodded solemnly. The berry was also poisonous. 'Not good,' he said.

'Wuh,' said the banderbear, leaping to its feet. 'Wuh-wuh-wuh!' it cried, and jumped up and down, up and down. And, as it continued to pummel and pound the offending berry, the trampled vegetation all round was shredded and the ground beneath flew up in clouds of dust. Tears of laughter streamed down Twig's face.

'It's OK,' he said. 'I promise.'

The banderbear came over and patted Twig gently on the head. 'Wu . . . wu . . . Fr . . . wuh. Fr-uh-nz,' it said.

'That's right,' Twig smiled. 'Friends.' He pointed to himself again. 'Twig,' he said. 'Say it. Twig.'

'T-wuh-g,' said the banderbear and beamed proudly. 'T-wuh-g! T-wuh-g! T-wuh-g!' it said, over and over, and it stooped down, seized the boy and swung him up onto its shoulders. Together, they lurched off into the darkening woods.

It wasn't long before Twig was foraging for himself. He wasn't as skilful as the banderbear with its giant claws and sensitive nose, but he learned quickly and the Deepwoods gradually became a less frightening place. All the same, in the dark black night, it was a comfort to feel the great heaving bulk of the banderbear beside him, its gruff snores soothing him back to sleep.

Twig thought about his woodtroll family less and less. He hadn't forgotten them exactly, it was just that there didn't seem any need to think much about anything. Eat, sleep, eat some more . . .

Every now and then, though, Twig was jolted out of the Deepwoods dream, once when he saw a sky ship in the distance, and a few times when he thought he saw the caterbird in the dappled branches of lullabee trees.

But life went on. They ate and slept and yodelled at the moon. And then it happened.

It was a crisp autumnal evening, and Twig was once again up on the banderbear's shoulders. They were searching out a sleeping place for the night when suddenly, out of the corner of his eye, Twig saw a flash of orange. He glanced round. Some way behind them was a small furry creature, like a ball of orange fluff.

A little further on and Twig looked round for a second time. Now there were four of the fluffy little creatures, all frisking about like hammelhorn lambs.

'Sweet,' he said.

'Wuh?' said the banderbear.

'Behind us,' Twig said, tapping the banderbear on the shoulder and pointing back.

The pair of them turned. By now there were a dozen of the curious animals, all bouncing along after them. When it caught sight of the creatures, the banderbear's ears began swivelling round and round, and from its mouth came a soft but high-pitched squeal.

'What is it?' said Twig and chuckled. 'You're not going to tell me you're frightened of *them*!'

The banderbear only squealed all the louder, and trembled from the ends of its ears to the tips of its toes. It was all Twig could do to hold on.

'Wig-wig!' the banderbear bellowed.

As Twig watched, the number of fluffy orange

creatures doubled, then doubled again. They scampered about in the twilight glow, this way and that, but never getting any nearer. The banderbear grew more and more agitated. It shuffled about nervously from foot to foot, squealing all the while.

Suddenly, it had had enough. 'Wuh-wuh!' it cried.

Twig gripped the banderbear's long hair and held on tightly as it lurched forwards. It trundled blindly through the forest. *Bump, bump, bump.* It was all Twig could do not to fall off. He glanced behind him. There was no doubt about what was happening: the orange balls of fluff were giving chase.

Twig's own heart was racing now. On their own the little creatures had looked sweet, but as a group there was something curiously menacing about them.

Faster and faster, the banderbear ran. It crashed through the woods, flattening everything before it. Time and again, Twig had to duck down behind its huge head as branches and bushes came hurtling towards him. The wig-wigs simply followed the path the great beast was carving – and it wasn't long before the ones at the front were catching up.

Twig looked down anxiously. Four or five of the creatures were now leaping at the banderbear's feet every time they touched the ground. Suddenly one of them clung on.

'Sky above!' Twig gasped as the fluffy ball split in half and two rows of savage teeth like the jags on a bear trap sprang into view. The next instant the teeth slammed shut on the banderbear's leg.

'Wuh-ooooo!' it screeched.

With Twig still clinging on for grim death, the banderbear leaned over, tore the wig-wig off, and tossed it away. The ferocious little beast rolled back over the ground, only to be replaced by four more.

'Squash them! Crush them!' Twig screamed.

But it was hopeless. No matter how many of the wig-wigs the banderbear sent flying through the air, there were always a dozen or more to take their place. They clung to its legs, to its arms; they crawled up its back towards the banderbear's neck, up towards Twig!

'Help me!' he screamed.

The banderbear jerked abruptly upright and stumbled over to a tall tree. Twig felt its huge paws round his waist as it pulled him from its shoulders and placed him high up into the branches of the tree, far out of reach of the bloodthirsty wig-wigs.

'T-wuh-g,' it said. 'Fr-uh-nz.'

'You climb up too,' said Twig. But as he looked back into the banderbear's sad eyes, he knew that would never be possible.

The wig-wigs bit into the banderbear's legs again and again until finally with a low moan, the huge beast toppled down to the ground. Its body was immediately covered with the vicious creatures.

Twig's eyes filled with tears. He turned away, unable to look. He clamped his hands over his ears but couldn't shut out the cries of the banderbear as it battled on.

Then the Deepwoods fell silent. Twig knew it was all over.

'Oh, banderbear,' he sobbed. 'Why? Why? Why?'

He wanted to jump down, knife unsheathed, and kill every single one of the wig-wigs. He wanted to avenge the death of his friend. Yet he knew all too well that there was not a thing he could do.

Twig wiped his eyes and looked down. The wig-wigs had gone. And of the banderbear, there wasn't a trace to be seen, not a bone, not a tooth or claw, not a single scrap of mossy fur. From far away there came the forlorn yodelling call of a distant banderbear. Time after time its heartrending cry echoed through the trees.

Twig held the tooth around his neck tightly in his hand. He sniffed. 'It can't answer you now,' he whispered tearfully. 'Or ever again.'

.CHAPTER NINE.

THE ROTSUCKER

Twig stared down into the twilight shadows beneath him. He couldn't see any of the wig-wigs. They had co-ordinated their deadly attack in silence, neither squeaking nor squealing throughout the entire operation. The only sound to be heard had been the crunching of bones and slurping of blood. Now the vicious little beasts had slipped away silently and were gone.

At least, Twig *hoped* they were gone. He sniffed again, and wiped his nose on his sleeve. He couldn't afford to be wrong.

Above his head the sky turned from brown to black. The moon rose, low and luminous. The stillness of dusk had already been broken by the first stirrings of the night creatures and now as Twig continued to sit and stare, unable to move, those sounds of night-time grew. They

whooped and wailed, they shuffled and screeched: invisible but no less perceptible for that. In the darkness you see with your ears.

Below Twig's swinging legs the forest floor steamed. A fine coiling mist wove itself round and around the trunks of the trees. It was as if the Deepwoods were simmering; with peril, with evil.

'I'll stay up here,' Twig whispered to himself as he pulled himself to his feet. 'Till morning.'

With his arms outstretched for balance, Twig made his way along the branch to the trunk of the tree. There he began to climb. Higher and higher he went, looking for some configuration of branches that would both support his weight and offer some comfort in the long night ahead.

As the leaves around him grew denser, Twig's eyes began to sting and water. He plucked a leaf and looked at it carefully. It was angular and glowed a pale turquoise. 'Oh, banderbear,' he sighed. 'Of all the trees you could have chosen, why did you have to place me in a lullabee tree?'

There was no point climbing any further. The upper branches of the lullabees were notoriously brittle. What was more, it was cold so high up. The biting wind was turning his exposed arms and legs to gooseflesh. Twig shifted round to the far side of the trunk and started back down again.

Abruptly, the moon disappeared. Twig paused. The moon remained hidden and the wind plucked at his fingers. Slowly, slowly, guided by the touch of the rough bark on his feet, Twig climbed carefully down. Wig-wigs or no wig-wigs, one slip and he'd crash down to certain death below.

With both hands gripping tightly to the branch by his head, and his left foot, leg bent at the knee, resting in a knothole in the trunk, Twig eased himself down. Droplets of cold sweat beaded his brow as his right foot probed the darkness for somewhere to stand.

Lower and lower he stretched. His arms ached. His

left leg felt as though it was about to be torn from its socket. Twig was on the point of giving up when, all at once, the very tip of his big toe found what it had been looking for: the next branch down.

'At last,' Twig whispered.

He relaxed his elbows, released his toegrip in the knothole and swung down till both feet landed on the branch. His toes sank deep into something soft and fluffy.

'No!' he yelped, and recoiled in horror.

There was something on the branch. An animal of some kind. Perhaps the wig-wigs were able to climb trees after all.

Kicking out blindly, Twig tried his best to pull himself back up to the safety of the branch above his head. But it was no use. He was tired. He heaved himself up, only to find his arms were too weak to take him quite far enough. His hands were beginning to lose their grip.

Suddenly, the moon burst brightly through the forest canopy. It sent flickering silver darts shooting down between the windblown leaves. Kite-shaped patterns of light played on the tree trunk, on the suspended body of Twig, and on the forest floor, far, far below him.

Twig felt his sharp chin pressing hard against his chest as he strained to see directly beneath him. His eyes confirmed what his toes had told him. There was something – *two somethings* – on the rough bark. They were clinging to the branch like the furry paws of some great beast which was climbing up to get him.

Tentatively, Twig lowered his legs and prodded them

with his toes. They were cold. They did not move.

Twig eased himself lower onto the broad branch and crouched quickly down. Close up, the two objects were not furry at all. They looked more like two balls of gossamer thread that had been wound round and round the branch. Twig inspected beneath the branch. His body quivered with excitement.

There, suspended from a silken rope, was a cocoon. Now Twig had seen cocoons before. Taghair slept in one, and he had been present in the lullabee grove when the caterbird had hatched. He had never, however, been so near to one. The long pendulous object was larger, and far more beautiful, than he had ever imagined.

'Amazing,' he whispered.

Woven from the finest filaments of thread, the cocoon looked as if it had been spun from sugar. It was broad and bulbous, and shaped like a giant woodpear which, as it swayed to and fro in the wind, glistened in the moonlight.

Twig reached down under the branch and grasped the silken rope. Then, taking care not to slip in his eagerness, he slid over the edge and lowered himself, hand over hand, until he was sitting astride the cocoon itself.

It felt like nothing Twig had ever felt before: soft to the touch – impossibly soft – but firm enough to hold its shape. And as Twig plunged his fingers into the thick silky wadding, a sweet and spicy fragrance rose up all around him.

A sudden gust of wind sent the cocoon twisting round. Above him, the brittle branches whistled and

cracked. Twig gasped and clutched hold of the rope. He looked down giddily at the dappled forest floor far below him. Something was there, scratching about noisily in the dead leaves. He could neither go up, nor down.

'But then I don't need to,' Twig said to himself. 'I can spend the night in the caterbird cocoon.' And as he spoke the words, his entire body tingled. He remembered the caterbird's words: *Taghair sleeps in our cocoons and dreams our dreams.* 'Perhaps,' Twig whispered excitedly, 'I, too, might dream their dreams.'

Mind made up, Twig twisted himself round until he was facing the cocoon. His nose pressed against the springy down. The sweet, spicy smell grew more intense and, as he lowered himself still further, the silken cocoon caressed his cheek. Finally, his feet came to rest on the matted rim, where the emerging caterbird had rolled back the fabric of the cocoon.

'Ready, steady . . . go!' said Twig.

He let go of the rope and dropped inside. The cocoon swung wildly for an instant. Twig closed his eyes, petrified that the rope would not hold. The swaying stopped. He opened his eyes again.

It was warm inside the cocoon – warm and dark and reassuring. Twig's heart ceased its frantic pounding. He breathed deeply of the aromatic perfume and was overwhelmed by a feeling of well-being. Nothing could hurt him now.

Twig curled himself up into a ball, knees bent and one arm folded beneath his head, and sank down into the padded softness. It was like being immersed in warm, scented oil. He felt snug, he felt safe and secure, he felt sleepy. His tired limbs grew heavy. His eyelids slowly closed.

'Oh, banderbear,' he whispered drowsily. 'Of all the trees you could have chosen, thank Sky you placed me in a lullabee tree.'

And, as the wind rocked the wonderful cocoon gently to and fro, to and fro, to and fro, Twig drifted off to sleep.

By the middle of the night, the clouds had all disappeared, carried away on winds, which had themselves
now dropped. The moon was once again low in the sky.
Far away in the distance, a sky ship, sails all hoisted to
catch the sluggish air, sailed across the moonlit night.

The leafy surface of the Deepwoods canopy sparkled
like water under the moon's glow. All at once a shadow
passed across it: the shadow of a flying creature which
glided low over the top of the forest.

It had broad and powerful black leathery wings,
scalloped at the back and tipped with vicious claws. The
very air seemed to tremble as the wings flapped,
ponderous yet purposeful, across the indigo sky. The
creature's head was small, scaly and where the mouth
should have been a long tubular snout stuck out. It
slurped and snuffled, and a foul-smelling vapour puffed
into the air with every wing-beat.

Little light from the sinking moon penetrated the
forest now, but the creature was not deterred. Raised
brassy-yellow eyes cast two wide beams of light which
scoured the shadowy depths. Round and around it flew,
back and forth. It would not give up until it found what
it had come for.

Suddenly its luminous eyes locked on to something
hanging from the branch of a tall turquoise lullabee:
something large and rounded and glistening. The
creature let out a piercing squawk, folded its wings and
crashed down through the forest canopy. Then, with its

strong stubby legs extended, it landed heavily on the branch of the tree and hunkered down. It cocked its head to one side and listened.

The sound of gentle breathing floated up towards it. It sniffed at the air and its whole body trembled with anticipation. It took a step forward. Then another. And another.

Designed for flight, the creature walked slowly, clumsily, gripping hold with one clawed foot before releasing the next. It walked right round the massive branch until it was hanging upside down.

With its talons digging into the rough bark above it, the creature's head was level with the opening to the cocoon. It poked inside it and prodded around with the bony tip of its long, hollow snout. It trembled again, more violently than before, and from deep down inside its body came a gurgling sound. Its stomach convulsed and a stream of bilious liquid spurted out of the end of its snout. Then it withdrew.

The yellow-green liquid fizzed where it landed and gave off twists of vapour. Twig screwed up his nose, but did not wake. In his dreams he was lying in a meadow beside a babbling, crystal-clear brook. Crimson poppies swayed back and forwards, filling the air with a smell so sweet it left him breathless.

Talons still firmly gripping the branch, the creature turned its attention to the cocoon itself. Filament by filament, it teased apart the matted clumps of wadding around the opening with the claws on its wings. It drew them silently across the hole. Quickly, the opening was closed.

Twig's eyelids fluttered. He was in a cavernous hallway now, lined with diamonds and emeralds which sparkled like a million eyes.

The creature flapped its wings and seized the branch in its wing-claws. It let go with its feet and then, suspended in mid-air, manoeuvred itself along the branch until its body was directly over the top of the cocoon. It splayed its legs and began sucking in air noisily. As it did so, its stomach inflated and the scales at the base of its abdomen stood up on end. Beneath each one was a rubbery pink duct which, as the creature continued to gulp at the air, slowly opened up.

All at once it grunted, and a sharp spasm juddered through its body. From the ducts, powerful jets of a sticky black substance squirted down onto the cocoon.

'Mffll-bnn,' Twig mumbled in his sleep. 'Mmmsh . . .'

The glutinous tar-like liquid soaked in and slid down over the cocoon in all directions, soon covering it com-

pletely.
When it
set, the
cocoon
became an
impenetrable
prison.

With a reedy
squawk of triumph,
the creature seized
the pod it had made
in its taloned feet,
sliced through the
silken rope with
one of its wing-
claws, and soared
off into the night.
Silhouetted against the
violet sky, the creature's huge
wings beat up and down; below it the deadly pod
swayed back and forwards, back and forwards.

Twig was floating on a raft in the middle of a sapphire
sea. The sun, warm and yellow, beat down on his face as
he bobbed along over the waves. All of a sudden, a ridge
of black clouds cut out the light. The sea grew rougher,
and rougher still.

Twig snapped his eyes open. He stared round him
wildly. It was black. Pitch black. He lay there, motion-
less, unable to make sense of what was happening. His
eyes refused to grow accustomed to the dancing dark-

ness. There was no light. Not a glimmer. A bolt of terror zinged in his head and shot down his spine.

'What's going on?' he screamed. 'Where's the opening?'

Struggling round to a crouching position, Twig felt about the surrounding casing with trembling fingers. It was hard to the touch. It echoed when knocked – *boom, boom, boom* – impervious to his pounding fists.

'Let me out,' he screamed. 'LET ME OUT!'

The rotsucker screeched and lurched to one side as the sudden movement inside the pod knocked it off balance. It beat its wings powerfully and gripped the matt black ridges all the more firmly in its talons. It was used to its quarry struggling to escape. The frantic jerks and jolts would soon subside. They always did.

Twig was beginning to pant. Stinging sweat ran down into his eyes. The acrid smell of bile clung to him like a second skin. He gagged. The darkness seemed to spin. He opened his mouth and a loose vomit gushed forth. It was fruity, sour, full of pips and seeds. A picture came to him of the banderbear handing him something delicious; the banderbear that had been devoured by the horrible wig-wigs. Twig opened his mouth again and his whole body convulsed. *Whooaarrsh!* The vomit splashed against the curved walls of Twig's prison and slopped around his feet.

The rotsucker shifted the juddering pod round in its talons again. The feathery lightness of dawn was already fanning out across the far horizon. Soon be back. Soon be home, little one. Then you can take your place with the others in my treetop store.

Choking. Heaving. Eyes streaming in the acrid blackness. Head pounding with the lack of air. Twig pulled his naming knife from his belt and gripped it tightly. Leaning forward on his knees, he began stabbing in a frenzy at the casing in front of him. The knife slipped round. Twig paused and wiped his sweaty palm down his trousers.

The knife had served him well already – against the hover worm, against the tarry vine – but would the steel blade be strong enough to shatter the shell? He slammed the point hard against the casing. It had to be. Again. And again. It just *had* to be.

Ignoring the jolts and judders which came from inside the pod, the rotsucker kept on towards its lofty store. It could already see the other pods silhouetted against the light, high up in the skeletal trees. Struggle away, my supper-lugs. The greater the struggle, the sweeter the soup, and the sound of the rotsucker's wheezy chortle echoed through the darkness. Soon you will fall as still as all the rest.

And when that happened, the evil-smelling bile the rotsucker had squirted into the cocoon would get to work. It would digest the body, turning the flesh and bones to slimy liquid. After a week, five days if the weather was warm, the rotsucker would drill a hole in the top of the pod with the serrated circle of hard bone at the end of its snout, insert the long tube and suck up the rich fetid stew.

'Break, break, break,' Twig muttered through gritted

teeth as he slammed his naming knife against the casing over and over and over again. Then, just as he was about to give up, the pod resounded with a loud crack as the casing finally gave. A chunk of shell the size of a plate fell away into the darkness.

'YES!' Twig screamed.

Air, fresh air, streamed in through the hole. Gasping with exhaustion, Twig leaned forwards, placed his face to the hole and gulped deeply. In out, in out. His head began to clear.

The air tasted good.

It tasted of life.

Twig peered ahead. Far away in front of him, a row of jagged dead pines stood black against the pink sky. At the top of one of the trees a clutch of egg-shaped objects lined a branch: they were sealed caterbird cocoons.

'Got to make the hole bigger,' Twig told himself as he raised the knife high above his head. 'And quickly.' He brought it down hard against the casing. It landed with an unfamiliar thud. 'What the . . . ?' He looked down and groaned.

The blow which had broken through the rock-hard shell had also shattered the blade of the knife. All he was holding was the handle. 'My naming knife,' said Twig, choking back the tears. 'Broken.'

Tossing the useless piece of bone aside, Twig leant against the back of the pod and began kicking viciously at the casing.

'Break, Sky damn you!' he roared. 'BREAK!'

The rotsucker wobbled in mid-flight. What's going on now, eh? My, my, what a determined supper-lugs you are. Let me just shift you round a little. There. That's better. Wouldn't want to drop you, would we?'

Twig kicked harder than ever. The pod echoed with the sounds of splintering shell and falling fragments. Suddenly, two wide cracks zigzagged across the casing, the warm glow of morning fuzzing their edges.

'Aaaii!' he shrieked. 'I'm falling.'

The rotsucker screeched with fury as the pod lurched. It found itself tumbling down through the air. Keep still, curse you! Beating its tired wings fiercely it pulled itself out of the plummeting spiral. But something was wrong. It knew that now. What are you playing at, my naughty little supper-lugs? You should be dead by now. But be sure I shan't let you go.

161

Twig kicked again, and the crack ripped over his head and round behind his back. Again, and it continued below him. He glanced down. There was a jagged line of light between his legs. The vomit and bile drained away.

Whatever happened now, the rotsucker was bound to go hungry. The pod was disintegrating. Its quarry would never putrefy.

Twig stared in horror at the crack below him, as the smear of green grew wider. He stopped kicking. Falling from this height would be too dangerous. More than ever before, he needed help. 'Caterbird,' he shrieked. 'Where are you?'

The rotsucker wheezed. Bad supper-lugs! Bad! It was almost at the end of its strength, sinking lower in the sky. Its brassy-yellow eyes swivelled round to look at its tree-top store. So near and yet so far.

Beneath him, the smudge turned from green to brown. Twig looked more closely. The forest had thinned out and, in parts, died. Long bleached skeletons of trees littered the glittering ground. Some were still standing, their dead branches reaching upwards, grasping at the air like bony fingers.

All at once there was a tremendous crash. The pod had hit the top of one of those dead branches. Twig was thrown back. His head smashed against the shell. The crack widened, and the pod, with Twig still in it, was falling.

Down, down, down. Twig's stomach churned. His heart was in his mouth. He closed his eyes, took a deep breath and braced himself for impact.

SQUELLLP!

He had landed in something soft, something which, even now, was oozing in between the cracks in the shell like grainy liquid chocolate. He dipped his finger in the brown substance and put it tentatively to his nose. It was mud. Thick peaty mud. He was in the middle of a boggy swamp.

Wobbling awkwardly, Twig reached up, slipped his fingers between the largest of the cracks, and tugged. The mud was already up to his ankles. At first nothing happened. Even now, the tar soaked fibres of the cocoon were formidably strong. The mud reached Twig's knees.

'Come *on*!' he said.

With his elbows locked, he prised the crack a little further apart. The veins stood out on his temples, his muscles knotted. Abruptly, light came streaming down on him. The shell had finally split in two.

'Oh, no,' he cried, as the larger piece of the broken pod immediately turned up on its end and slipped down into the mud. 'Now what?'

His only hope lay with the smaller piece, still floating on the surface. If he could just climb up, maybe he could use it as a makeshift boat.

In the sky above him he heard a shrill shriek of fury. He looked up. There, circling above his head, was a hideous and repulsive creature. It was watching him through gleaming blank yellow eyes. Broad black leathery wings, glistening with sweat, flapped noisily into the air. Suddenly, it turned and dived, and the next instant Twig felt sharp talons grazing his head and pulling out tufts of hair by the roots.

The creature wheeled round and dived again. Rubbery threads of green saliva were streaming down from the end of its long snout. This time, Twig ducked. As it swooped in close, it screeched again and sprayed him with a shower of the evil-smelling bile.

Gagging emptily, Twig heard the fading clap-clap of wings. The vile creature was flapping away. When he looked up again it was perched at the top of a distant dead tree, black against the curdled morning sky. Beneath it, hung the cluster of pods, each one full of rotting matter. Twig sighed with relief. The creature had given up. He would not be joining the others in that line of death.

A moment later, his relief turned to panic. 'I'm sinking!' he cried out.

Clutching the piece of shell, Twig tried desperately to heave himself up out of the bog. But each time he pulled down, the shell tipped over, taking on still more of the mud. At his third attempt, it sank completely.

The mud was round his stomach now, and rising. He flailed his arms about and kicked out with his legs, but the thick ooze only sucked him deeper down.

'Oh, Gloamglozer!' Twig wailed. 'What do I do?'

'Don't panic, that's the important thing,' came a voice.

Twig gasped. There was someone there, watching him struggle. 'Help!' he screamed. 'HELP ME!'

He twisted himself round as best he could, a movement which lost him another couple of inches. Past his chest now, the mud was creeping up to the base of his neck. A short bony goblin with a flat head and yellow skin was leaning up against a dead tree, chewing a piece of straw.

'You want *me* to help *you*?' it said, its voice sing-song and nasal.

'Yes. Yes, I do. You've got to help me,' he said, and spluttered as the mud trickled into his mouth and down his throat.

The goblin smirked and tossed the straw aside. 'Then I shall, Master Twig,' it said. 'So long as you're sure.'

It reached up, snapped a dead branch from the tree and held it out across the treacherous swamp. Twig spat the foul mud from his mouth and made a lunge for it. He grasped hold of the bleached wood and clung on for dear life.

The goblin pulled. Twig was dragged through the thick sucking mud, closer and closer to the bank. He spat. He spluttered. He prayed the branch would not break. All at once he felt solid ground beneath his knees, then his elbows. The goblin let the branch drop and Twig crawled out of the swamp.

Free at last, Twig collapsed. And there he lay, exhausted, face down in the dusty earth. He owed his life to the goblin. Yet when he finally lifted his head to thank his rescuer, he found himself once more alone. The flat-head was nowhere to be seen.

'Hey,' Twig called weakly. 'Where are you?'

There was no answer. He pulled himself to his feet and looked about him. The goblin had gone. All that remained was the piece of straw, chewed at one end, which lay on the ground. Twig crouched down beside it. 'Why did you run off?' he murmured.

He sat down in the dust and hung his head. All at once he was struck by another question. How had the flat-head goblin known his name?

CHAPTER TEN

THE TERMAGANT TROGS

It was still. The sun beat down, hot and bright. All the vomiting in the sealed pod had left Twig's throat feeling as if it had been sandpapered. He needed a drink.

He picked himself up and looked back at his shadow which stretched far out across the treacherous swamp. At the end of it lay still water. It sparkled tantalizingly. If only there was some way of getting to it without being sucked down into the mud. Twig spat and turned away again.

'It's probably stagnant anyway,' he muttered.

He stomped off across the spongy wasteland. The swamp had once extended this far. Now, apart from the occasional patch of pale-green algae, nothing grew. Yet there was life there. With every step Twig took, clouds of vicious woodmidges flew up and buzzed round him. They landed on his face, his arms, his legs –

and where they landed, so they bit.

'Get off! Get away!' Twig cried as he slapped at the voracious insects. 'If it's not one thing, it's . . . YOUCH!' Slap. '. . . another!' Slap. Slap. Slap.

Twig started to run. The woodmidges flew with him, like satin sheets flapping in the wind. Faster. Faster. Past the bony skeletons of dead trees. Headlong over the bouncy peat. Stumbling, slipping, but never stopping. Out of the desolate home of the evil rotsucker, and back to the Deepwoods.

Twig smelled them before he reached them. The loamy soil, the luxuriant foliage, the succulent fruit – familiar scents that set his mouth watering and his heart clopping faster than ever. The woodmidges were less impressed. As the rich and fertile smells grew stronger, so their numbers dropped. They abandoned their quarry and returned to the wasteland, where the air was pungent and sour.

Twig trudged onwards and upwards. The Deepwoods wrapped themselves around him like a vast green quilt. There were no tracks, no paths; he had to carve his own way through the lush undergrowth. Through woodfern and bullbracken he went, up slopes and down dips. When he came to a sallowdrop tree, he stopped.

The sallowdrop, with its long waving fronds of pearly leaves, only grew near water. The banderbear had taught him that. Twig pushed aside the beaded curtains of the hanging branches, and there, babbling along over a bed of pebbles, was a stream of crystal clear water.

'Thank Sky,' Twig rasped and fell to his knees. He cupped his hands and dipped them in the ice-cold water. He took a sip, swallowed, and felt the cold liquid coursing down inside his body. It tasted good; earthy and sweet. He drank more, and more. He drank until his stomach was full and his thirst was quenched. Then, with a grateful sigh, Twig dropped down into the stream with a splash.

And there he lay. The water ran over him, soothing the woodmidge bites, cleaning his clothes and hair. He remained there until every trace of mud and vomit and stinking bile had been washed away.

'Clean again,' he said, and pulled himself back onto his knees.

All at once, a flash of orange darted across the water. Twig froze. Wig-wigs were orange! Head still bowed, Twig raised his eyes and peered nervously through his lank and dripping hair.

Crouched down behind a rock on the far side of the stream was not a wig-wig but a girl. A girl with pale, almost translucent skin and a shock of orange hair. Company.

'Hey!' Twig called out. 'I . . .' But the girl darted out of sight. Twig leapt to his feet. 'OY!' he yelled as he splashed across the stream. Why wouldn't she wait? He leaped up the bank and onto the rock. Some way ahead, he noticed the girl dodging behind a tree. 'I won't hurt you,' he panted to himself. 'I'm nice. Honest!'

By the time he reached the tree, however, the girl was gone again. He saw her glance back before slipping into a glade of swaying greatgrass. Twig dashed in after her. He wanted her to stop, to come back, to talk to him. On and on he ran. Around trees, across clearings – always close, but never quite close enough.

As she raced behind a broad and ivy-clad trunk, the girl looked back for a third time. Twig felt the hairs at the nape of his neck stand on end; his hammelhornskin waistcoat bristled. What if the girl wasn't checking to see whether she had given him the slip? What if she was making sure that he was still following?

He kept on, but more cautiously now. Round the tree he went. The girl was nowhere to be seen. Twig looked up into the branches. His heart was hammering, his scalp tingled. There could be anything hiding up in the dense foliage waiting to pounce – anything at all.

He fingered his amulets. He took another step forwards. Where *was* the girl? Was it all just another horrible trap . . . ?

'Waaaaiii!' Twig screamed.

The ground had opened up and Twig was falling. Into the earth he tumbled, and down a long curving tunnel. Bump, bump, roll, bumpety, roll, crash, bang and *plaff*, down onto a thick bed of soft straw.

Twig looked up, dazed. Everything was spinning. Yellow lights, twisted roots – and four faces staring down at him.

'Where you bin?' two of them were saying. 'You know I don't like you going upground. It's too dangerous. You'll get carried off by the gloamglozer one day, my girl, and that's a fact.'

'I can look after myself,' the other two replied sulkily.

Twig shook his head. The four faces became two. The larger one loomed closer, all bloodshot eyes and corrugated lips.

'And what's this?' it complained. 'Oh, Mag, what have you brought back *now*?'

The pale-skinned girl stroked Twig's hair. 'It followed me home, Mumsie,' she said. 'Can I keep it?'

The older woman pulled her head away and folded her arms, breathing in, and swelling up, as she did so. She stared at Twig suspiciously. 'I trust he's not a *talker*,' she said. 'I've told you before, I draw the line at pets that can talk.'

Twig swallowed anxiously.

Mag shook her head. 'I don't think so, Mumsie. The occasional noise, but no words.'

Mumsie grunted. 'You'd better be telling me the truth. Talkers means trouble.'

Mumsie was enormous, with rippling forearms and a neck as broad as her head. What was more, unlike the girl, whose pale skin made her almost invisible in the subterranean gloom, Mumsie was all too visible. With the exception of her face, almost every bit of exposed skin was covered with iridescent tattoos.

There were trees, weapons, symbols, animals, faces, dragons, skulls; you name it. Even her bald head had been tattooed. What Twig had first taken for curls of hair plastered to her scalp, were in fact coiled snakes.

She reached up and scratched thoughtfully under her broad nose, inadvertently flexing her biceps as she did so. The sleeve of her patterned dress rode up with a rustle – and Twig found himself staring at a picture of a young girl with fiery orange hair. Beneath it, in indigo letters, was a tattooed message: MUMSIE LOVES MAG.

'Well?' said Mag.

Her mother sniffed. 'Mag,' she said, 'you can be such a trying trog at times. But . . . I suppose so,' she said. 'HOWEVER,' she added, interrupting Mag's whoops of delight, *'you're* responsible for it. Do you understand? *You* feed it, *you* exercise it, and if it makes a mess in the cavern, *you* clean it up. Do I make myself clear?'

'Crystal clear, Mumsie,' said Mag.

'And if I hear so much as a single word,' she went on, 'I'll wring its scrawny little neck. Right?'

Mag nodded. She reached forwards and grabbed Twig by the hair. 'Come on,' she said.

'Yow!' Twig helped, and slapped her hand away.

'It hit me,' Mag howled at once. 'Mumsie, my pet hit me – it *hurt* me!'

Twig suddenly felt himself being whisked up off the floor and swung round. He stared petrified into the trog-woman's ferocious bloodshot eyes. 'If you ever, EVER push, slap, scratch or bite my little moonbeam, I'll—'

'Or in any other way hurt my body,' Mag butted in.

'Or in any other way hurt her body, I'll—'

'*Or* my feelings.'

'— hurt her body or her feelings, I'll—'

'Or try to run away . . .'

'Or try to run away,' Mumsie repeated. 'You're dead!' Her paper dress rustled as she shook him. 'Obedient and dumb, that's the rule. OK?'

Twig didn't know whether to nod or not. If he wasn't allowed to speak, was he expected to understand? With Mumsie's massive fist gripping his coat so tightly, he could scarcely move anyway. She sniffed, and dropped him onto the floor.

Twig looked up warily. Mag was standing behind her mother, her hands held primly at her front. Her face bore an expression of impossible smugness. She leant forwards and tugged his hair for a second time. Wincing with pain, Twig climbed passively to his feet.

'That's more like it,' Mumsie growled. 'What are you going to call it?' she said.

Mag shrugged and turned to her new pet. 'Have you got a name?' she said.

'Twig,' he replied automatically – and immediately wished he hadn't.

'What's that?' roared Mumsie. 'Was that a word?' She prodded Twig hard in the chest. 'Are you a talker after all?'

'Twigtwigtwigtwig,' he said, desperately trying to make it sound as unwordlike as possible. 'Twigtwigtwig!'

Mag put her arm around Twig's shoulders and smiled

up at her mother. 'I think I'll call him Twig.'

Mumsie glared at Twig through narrowed eyes. 'One word, that's all,' she snarled. 'And I'll rip your head off.'

'Twig's going to be just fine,' Mag reassured her. 'Come along, boy,' she said to him. 'Let's go and play.'

Mumsie stood, hands on hips, watching as Mag dragged him away. Twig kept his head down. 'I'll be keeping my eye on that one,' he heard her say. 'You see if I don't.'

As they continued along the tunnel, Mumsie's threats faded away. There were stairs and ramps and long narrow slopes that took them lower, always lower, deep down into the ground. Twig felt uneasy at the thought of the weight of all that earth and rock above him. What was to stop it falling down? What was to stop it swallowing him up?

All at once, the oppressive walkway came to an end. Twig stared round him, trembling with amazement. The pair of them were standing in an immense underground cavern.

Mag let go of his hair. 'You'll like it down here with us termagant trogs, Twig,' she was saying. 'It's never too hot, it's never too cold. There's no rain, no snow, no wind. There are no dangerous plants and no wild beasts . . .'

Twig's fingers moved automatically to the tooth around his neck, and a tear trickled down his cheek.

No dangerous plants and no wild beasts, he thought. But no sky, no moon . . . The girl prodded him roughly in the back, and Twig walked on. And no freedom.

177

Like the tunnels, the cavern glowed with a pale light. Below his feet, the ground had been trampled flat under generations of trogfeet. Above, the lofty ceiling towered far over his head. Spanning the two, like knobbly pillars, were long thick gnarled roots.

It's like a mirror-image of the Deepwoods themselves, he thought. But the Deepwoods of winter, when the trees are stripped and bare.

Bathed in the cavern's glow, the roots were gaunt and twisted and ... Twig gasped. He'd been wrong. The light wasn't shining *on* the tree roots, but *from* them.

'Twig!' barked Mag sternly, as he ran for a closer look.

White, yellow, mushroom-brown; at least half of the long thick roots were giving out a softly pulsing glow. Twig placed his hand against one. It was warm, and throbbed faintly.

'TWIG!' Mag screeched. 'HEEL!'

Twig looked round. Mag was glaring menacingly. Obedient and dumb, Twig remembered. He trotted over and stood by her side.

Mag patted him on the head. 'Interested in the roots, are you?' she said. 'They provide us with all we need.'

Twig nodded, but remained silent.

'Light, of course,' said Mag, pointing to the roots that glowed. 'Food,' and she broke off two nodules from some fibrous roots. One she popped into her mouth. The other she handed to Twig, who stared at it unenthusiastically. 'Eat!' said Mag insistently. 'Go on!' And when Twig still refused to put it in his mouth, she added sweetly, 'I'll tell Mumsie.'

The nodule was crunchy and juicy. It tasted of toasted nuts. 'Mmm-mmm,' Twig mumbled and licked his lips theatrically.

Mag smiled and moved on. 'These we dry and grind for flour,' she explained. 'These we pulp and turn into paper. These burn well. And this . . .' she began, stopping next to a bulbous flesh-coloured root. 'Strange,' she said, and frowned. 'I didn't know these grew wild.' She turned to Twig and looked him up and down. 'Twig,' she said sternly. 'You must never, *ever* eat this type of root.'

A little further on, they came to a place where most of the vertical roots had been cut, to form a clearing around a deep lake of dark water. Those roots which remained fanned out near the ground, domed and serpentine. In amongst them, was a collection of huge capsules, each one separate from, but connected to, its neighbour. Rounded, buff-coloured and with small dark circular entrances, the capsules formed a mound up to five storeys high in places.

'The trogcombs are where we live,' said Mag. 'Follow me.'

Twig smiled to himself. Mag hadn't grabbed him by the hair. She was beginning to trust him.

The capsules, Twig discovered, were made of a thick papery substance, like Mumsie's dress, only thicker. It cracked under his feet as Twig stumbled up the inter-connecting walkways, and echoed hollowly when he tapped on the round walls.

'Don't do that!' said Mag sharply. 'It annoys the neigh-bours.'

Mag's capsule was situated to the top left of the mound and was considerably larger inside than it looked from the outside. The light from the roots glowed creamily through the walls. Twig sniffed. There was a hint of cinnamon in the air.

'You must be tired,' Mag announced. 'Your place is over there,' she said, pointing to a basket. 'Mumsie doesn't like pets sleeping on my bed.' She grinned mischievously. 'But I do! Come on, up you jump,' she said, patting the end of the bed. 'I won't tell her if you don't,' she said and burst out laughing.

Twig did as he was told. Forbidden it might have been, but the thick papery mattress was soft and warm. Twig fell instantly into a deep and dreamless sleep.

Some hours later – day and night had no meaning in the constant glow of the trog dwellings – Twig woke to the feel of someone patting his head. He opened his eyes.

'Sleep well?' said Mag brightly.

Twig grunted.

'Good,' she said, jumping out of bed, 'coz we've got loads to do. We'll do a spot of nodule collecting and root-milk tapping for breakfast. Then, after we've cleaned up, Mumsie wants us to help with some paper making. So many of us girls have been turning termagant recently, they're running out of dress material.

'And then if you're good,' Mag continued without taking a breath, 'we'll go walkies. But first of all,' she said, fiddling with his hair and running her fingers gently over his cheek. 'First of all, Twig darling, I'm going to make you look beautiful.'

Twig groaned, and watched miserably as Mag busied herself in a small cupboard. A moment later she was back, carrying a trayful of bits and pieces. 'There,' she said, placing it on the floor. 'Now come and sit in front of me.'

Reluctantly, Twig did as he was told.

Mag took a soft grey lump of spongy rootfibre and washed him with water she'd fetched from the lake earlier, and perfumed with roseroot. Next, she patted him dry and drenched him in a dark, spicy powder. When Twig sneezed, Mag wiped his running nose for him with a handkerchief.

It's the indignity of it all! Twig thought, as he turned his head angrily away.

'Now, now!' Mag chided him. 'We wouldn't want Mumsie to hear that you've been a naughty pet, would we?'

Twig fell still, and remained so as Mag picked up a wooden comb, and began to tease the tangles from his matted hair.

'You've got nice hair, Twig,' she said. 'Thick and black . . .' She tugged vigorously at a stubborn knot. 'But *very* tangled! Why under Earth did you let it get into this state?' She tugged again.

Twig winced. His eyes watered, and he bit into his lower lip until the blood came. But he didn't make a sound.

'*I* brush my hair twice a day,' said Mag, throwing back her bright orange mane with a toss of her head. She got closer to Twig. 'Soon,' she whispered, 'it will fall out. Every single hair. And then I, too, will turn termagant. Just like Mumsie.'

Twig nodded sympathetically.

'I can't wait!' Mag exclaimed, to his surprise. 'A termagant. Can you imagine, my little Twig, darling?' She lay the comb down. 'No,' she said, 'of course you can't. But then that's because you're a male. And males—'

She stopped to uncork a small bottle, and poured some thick yellow liquid into the palm of her hand. It was sweet, yet pungent, and as she rubbed it into Twig's hair his scalp tingled and his eyes began to smart.

'— can't be termagants.' She paused again. Then, selecting a small bunch of hair from the rest, she split it into three thin locks, and began to plait it. 'Mumsie says it's all because of the root. The Mother Bloodoak,' she said reverently.

Twig shuddered at the very mention of the blood-thirsty, flesh-hungry, tree, which had so nearly taken his own life. He stroked his hammelhornskin waistcoat gratefully.

'It's that pinky root we saw on our way here, Twig,' she went on as she threaded beads onto the finished braid. 'Do you remember? The one I told you never to eat. It's poisonous for males, you see? Deadly poisonous,' she said in a hushed whisper. 'Though not for us females,' she added.

Twig heard her chuckle as she separated a second bunch of hair.

'It's the rootsap that makes Mumsie and all the others so big and strong. "When the Mother Bloodoak courses red, the termagants shall all be fed." That's how the saying goes.'

Twig flinched. 'When the Mother Bloodoak courses red . . .' That was something he knew all about. His stomach churned queasily as Mag continued to braid and bead his hair.

'Ooh, you are beginning to look pretty, Twig,' said Mag. Twig grimaced. 'Of course,' she went on thoughtfully, 'the trog males aren't happy with the situation. Horrible, scrawny, sneaky, weedy, weasely individuals that they are,' she said, screwing up her nose in disgust. She sighed. 'Still, they have their uses. After all, *someone* has to cook and clean!'

Thank Sky I'm just a pet, thought Twig.

'They tried to sabotage everything once,' she went on. 'Before I was born. Apparently, all the males got together and tried to burn the Mother Bloodoak down. The termagants were furious. Beat them black and blue, they did. They haven't tried anything since!' she added, and laughed unpleasantly. 'Useless bunch of wasters!'

Twig felt three more beads being knotted into place.

'Anyway,' said Mag more quietly, 'these days the main roots are well guarded . . .' Her voice trailed away. 'There!' she announced. 'Turn round and let me look at you.'

Twig did so.

'Perfect!' she said. 'Come on, Twig, darling. Let's go and see about that breakfast.'

Time passed, as time does, though in the unchanging trog cavern it was difficult to tell how much. Certainly Mag seemed to be forever clipping the nails on his fingers and toes. And the last time she had groomed his hair she commented more than once on how long it had grown.

Pampered and petted by Mag and the other trog females, Twig's life with the termagants was pleasant enough. Yet he found the subterranean world oppressive. He missed fresh air and the bite of the wind. He missed sunrise and sunset. He missed the smell of rain, the sound of birdsong, the colour of the sky. Most of all, he missed the banderbear.

The curious thing about living underground – *beneath* the Deepwoods, with its terrors and dangers – was that it gave Twig time to think. With the banderbear, there had been no need to think at all. There was always food to be foraged; there were always sleeping places to be found. Now, with everything on hand, Twig had nothing to do *but* think.

When he had first arrived, Mag seldom let Twig out of her sight. Lately, however, the novelty of having a new pet seemed to have worn off. Mag had fitted him with a collar and taken to tethering him to her bed whenever she went out without him.

The rope was long enough for Twig to go anywhere he wanted within the papery capsule, and even allowed him to get half-way down the stairs outside. But each time he reached the end of the rope, and the collar tightened around his neck, Twig was reminded that he was a prisoner, and his heart longed to return to the Deepwoods above.

Perhaps he would finally find the path and return home to his family. Spelda would be overjoyed at her son returning from the Deepwoods. Even Tuntum might smile, clap him on the back and invite him on a tree-felling trip. Everything would be different. He'd fit in this time, try harder, he'd do what woodtrolls do, think woodtroll thoughts, and he'd never, *never*, stray from the path again.

The collar chafed his neck. Then again, he thought, wouldn't he be just as much a prisoner if he did go back? Forever trying to be like a woodtroll but never quite belonging.

He thought of the caterbird. What *had* become of it? 'So much for watching over me,' he muttered bitterly. *Your destiny lies beyond the Deepwoods*, it had told him. Twig snorted. 'Beyond!' he said. 'Beneath more like, with my destiny to remain the pampered pet of a spoilt child. Oh, Gloamglozer!' he cursed.

There was a rustling outside the trogcomb. Twig froze. I must stop talking to myself, he thought. One of these days, I'll be found out.

The next moment, Mag came bursting into the capsule. She had a folded length of brown paper over one arm. 'I've been told to prepare myself,' she announced excitedly.

She lay the paper out on the floor and began drawing. Twig nodded towards it and looked puzzled.

Mag smiled. 'Soon, Twig, darling,' she said. 'I will have this tattooed on my back.' Twig looked down at the picture with more interest. It was of a massive muscular termagant; legs apart, hands on hips, and with a ferocious expression on the face. 'We all do,' she explained.

Twig smiled weakly. He pointed to the picture, then at Mag herself and back at the picture.

'Yes,' said Mag. 'It's me. Or will be.'

Twig pointed to himself and cocked his head to one side.

'Oh, Twig,' she whispered gently. 'I'll *always* love you.'

Twig sat back, reassured. At that moment, however, there came from outside the sound of heavy footfalls. Twig's feeling of well-being dissolved and he began chewing the corner of his scarf. It was Mumsie.

'Mag?' she screeched. 'MAG!'

Mag looked up. 'I'm in here,' she called back, and the entrance was filled with the towering figure of Mumsie herself.

'You're to come with me,' she said to Mag. 'Now.'

'Is it time?' Mag asked eagerly.

'It's time,' came the gruff reply.

Mag leaped off the bed. 'Did you hear that, Twig? It's time! Come on.'

'You'll not need no pet where you're going,' said Mumsie.

'Oh, Mumsie, plee-ease!' Mag wheedled.

'I'm telling you, you won't want it there. Not after.'

'I will!' said Mag defiantly.

Twig looked from one to the other. Mumsie was scowling. Mag was smiling.

'You *would* like to come, wouldn't you?' she said.

Twig smiled back. Anything was better than more time spent tethered to the bed. He nodded his head vigorously up and down.

'You see,' said Mag triumphantly. 'I told you.'

Mumsie snorted. 'You credit that animal with far too much sense . . .'

'Please, Mumsie. Please!' Mag pleaded.

'Oh, if you must,' said Mumsie wearily, as she gathered up the painted paper. 'But you're to keep it on its lead.' She rounded on Twig and fixed him with her bloodshot glare. 'And woe betide you if you do anything – ANYTHING AT ALL – to spoil my Mag's big day!'

There was an air of expectation outside. The paths leading round the lake were thick with female trogs all heading in the same direction. Some were neighbours who Twig recognized. Some were strangers to him. 'See how far they've come,' said Mag delightedly.

On the far side of the lake, they came to a high fence which formed a vast circular enclosure. Clusters of the thin listless males hung round the guarded entrance. They cringed and whimpered as Mumsie cut a swathe through them.

'Stay close, Twig,' Mag snapped, and yanked at the lead.

Together, the three of them entered the enclosure. As they appeared, a roar of approval went up from the crowd assembled inside. Mag hung her head and smiled shyly.

Twig was greeted by a sight that he could scarcely believe was real. Extending down from far above his head was an enormous set of roots which fanned out near the ground to form an immense and lofty dome. Hand in hand around it stood the termagants, their tattooed skin bathed in the root's fleshy pink light.

Mumsie took hold of Mag's hand. 'Come,' she said.

''Ere!' said one of the guards. 'That creature can't enter the Inner Sanctuary.'

Mumsie noticed the lead still wound around Mag's other hand. 'Course it can't,' she said. She snatched the lead away and tied one end firmly to a twist of root. 'You can get it later,' she said, and chuckled throatily.

This time Mag made no move to stop her. As if in a trance, she stepped through the break in the circle of hands and on into the dome of roots itself. She didn't look back.

Twig peered through the gaps in the roots. At the very centre was the taproot. Thick and knobbly, it glowed brighter than all the rest. Mag – his little Mag – was standing with her back to it. Her eyes were closed. Suddenly the termagants began to chant.

> 'Oh! Ma-Ma Mother Bloodoak!
> Oh! Ma-Ma Mother Bloodoak!'

Over and over, louder and louder, they cried, until the entire cavern quaked with the deafening noise. Twig clamped his hands over his ears. In front of the taproot Mag had begun to squirm and writhe.

All at once, the cacophony came to an end. The silence trembled uncertainly. Twig watched as Mag turned to face the root. She raised her arms. She looked upwards.

'BLEED FOR ME!' she cried.

Before her voice had faded away, a sudden change came over the dome. The termagants gasped. Twig jumped away fearfully as the root he was tethered to abruptly changed colour. He looked round. The whole vast network of roots was glowing a deep and bloody crimson.

'Yes!' cried Mumsie, 'the time is indeed upon our daughter, Mag.'

She pulled a small object from the folds of her paper dress. Twig squinted to see. It looked like the tap from a barrel. She placed it against the pulsing red central root and hammered it home with her fist. Then, smiling at Mag, she pointed to the floor.

Mag knelt before the spout, raised her head and opened wide her mouth. Mumsie turned the spigot and a stream of frothing red liquid immediately gushed out. It splashed over her head and streamed down her back, her arms, her legs. Twig saw Mag's shoulders rising and falling in the crimson light.

'She's drinking it!' he shuddered.

Mag drank and drank and drank; she drank so much that Twig thought she must burst. Finally, she sighed a deep sigh and let her head fall forward. Mumsie switched off the flow of liquid. Mag climbed unsteadily to her feet. Twig gasped. The thin pale-skinned girl was beginning to expand.

Upwards, outwards, her whole body was growing larger. The flimsy dress she had been wearing split and fell to the ground – and still she grew. Massive shoulders, bulging biceps, tree-trunk legs ... And her head! It was already immense when, suddenly, the hair – that wild shock of orange – cascaded down to the ground. The transformation was complete.

'Welcome!' said Mumsie, wrapping the freshly painted dress around the newest termagant in the trog-cavern.

'Welcome!' cried the circle of her termagant sisters.

Mag turned slowly round in acknowledgement. Twig recoiled with fear. Where was the pale thin girl who had loved him and looked after him? Gone. In her place was a fearsome and terrible termagant trog. Once tattooed, she would look exactly like her mother, Mumsie.

Mag continued to look around. Their eyes met. She smiled. Twig smiled back. Perhaps she hadn't changed – inside, at least. A thick slobbering tongue, like a slab of liver, emerged from Mag's mouth and slurped over her corrugated lips. Her bloodshot eyes glinted.

'YOU LITTLE PIECE OF VERMIN!' she bellowed.

Twig looked over his shoulders in horror. Surely she couldn't be addressing him. Not her pet. Not her 'Twig, darling'. 'Mag!' he cried out. 'Mag, it's me!'

'Aaaargh!' screamed Mumsie. 'I *knew* he was a talker.'

'Yes,' said Mag coldly. 'But not for much longer.'

Twig felt the earth shaking as she pounded towards him. With trembling fingers he tugged at the knot. In vain. Mumsie had tied it far too tight. Twig gripped hold of the rope, placed both feet up against the root and

pressed back as hard as he possibly could. Nothing happened.

'Don't even think of escaping!' Mag roared.

Twig shifted his grip and tried again. There was a crack, and he flew back through the air. The rope had held – but not the root. A frothing red substance oozed from where it had severed.

'Whooooaaahhh!' Mag raged.

Twig turned on his heels and ran. He darted between two of the guards and sprinted down towards the lake. The trog males stood around gawping.

'Move!' Twig yelled as he elbowed them out of the way.

He could hear Mag behind him, followed closely by the rest of the termagants. 'Rip out his gizzards!' they were screeching. 'Tear off his legs! Smash him to smithereens!'

Twig reached the lake. He sped away to the left. A group of half a dozen trog males were standing in front of him.

'STOP HIM!' Mag ordered loudly. 'CATCH THE LITTLE BEAST!'

Then, louder still, when they simply stepped aside as Twig thundered past: 'YOU PATHETIC LITTLE MORONS!'

Twig glanced back over his shoulder. Mag was gaining on him. There was a look of terrible determination in her bloodshot eyes. Oh, Mag, he thought. What have you become?

Mag drew level with the trog males. They were watching her askance; all, that is, apart from one. As Mag lumbered past him, he stuck out his leg. It caught Mag's foot. She stumbled. She lurched. She lost her balance and

came crashing to the ground.

Twig gasped with surprise. It had been no accident.

Mag sprawled round and made a grab for the trog male, but he was too agile for her. He leaped to his feet, limped out of reach and looked up. Cupping his hands to his mouth, he called to Twig.

'What are you waiting for? Head for the roots where they shine brightest. Over in that direction.' There was a wheedling, mocking tone to his voice.

Twig looked round.

'Well?' the trog male gave a twisted smile. 'Do you want to be skinned alive by your little mistress? Follow the wind, pampered pet – and don't look back.'

CHAPTER ELEVEN

GARBLE, GABTROLL AND HEARTCHARMING

Twig did exactly as instructed. He ran headlong across the trog-cavern towards a distant point where the lights from the roots glowed brightest and not once did he look back. He could hear the furious termagants behind him, panting, pounding; sometimes catching up, sometimes falling behind.

As he neared the patch of brightness, it revealed itself to be a densely packed cluster of gleaming white roots. Which way now? His scalp tingled, his heart throbbed. There were half a dozen tunnels in front of him. Which one – if any – would lead him outside?

'He's lost!' he heard one of the termagants bellowing.

'Head him off,' instructed another.

'Then, off with his head!' roared yet another, and they all screeched with hideous laughter.

Twig was desperate. He would have to escape down

one of the tunnels but what if the one he chose was a dead end? And all the while he was trying to decide which one to take, the termagants were trundling closer. Any second they would bear down upon him. Then it would be too late.

Twig shuddered with fear and exhaustion. As he hurried past the entrance to one tunnel, a cold draught of air turned his sweating skin to gooseflesh. Of course! *Follow the wind*: the trog male's words. Without a second thought, Twig dashed down into the airy tunnel.

Wide at first, the opening soon grew both narrower and lower. Twig didn't mind. The more he had to stoop, the less likely it was that the huge termagants would be able to follow. He heard them, grunting and groaning and cursing their misfortune. All at once the tunnel turned a corner and came to an abrupt halt.

'Oh, what?' Twig groaned. It was a *real* dead end. He stared in horror at a pile of bleached bones which lay half covered by sand and shale. There was a skull, and the beaded remnants of plaited hair; a twist of rope was looped around the crumbling neck. It was a pet that had not managed to escape.

Just ahead of him, a single root extended down into the tunnel. Twig reached out his hand. It felt as dead as everything else; cold, stiff, and not shining. So where was the light coming from? He looked up, and there, far far above his head, was a small circle of silvery brilliance.

'He's found one of the air shafts,' came the furious voice of one of the termagants.

Twig pulled himself up into the branch-like growths of the root. 'Indeed I have,' he muttered.

Hand over foot over foot over hand he went, climbing towards the light. Arms aching and fingers trembling, he looked up again. The light seemed no nearer. A wave of alarm coursed through his body. What if the hole at the top wasn't large enough for him to climb through?

Foot over hand over hand over foot, higher and higher he continued, his breathing loud and rhythmical. Ooh. Aah. Ooh! Aah! At last, the circle of light did start to look bigger. Hurrying up the last few feet of root as quickly as he dared – it was a long way back down to the bones at the bottom of the shaft – Twig stretched his arm out into the warm sunlight.

'Thank Sky it's daytime,' he sighed. He heaved himself out onto the grass and rolled over. 'Otherwise I'd have never found my way ou . . .' Twig fell silent. He was not alone. The air was alive with panting, with snarling, with the juicy odour of decay. Slowly, he lifted his head.

Lolling tongues and flared black nostrils. Ice-pick teeth, bared, glinting, slavering. Yellow eyes, staring impassive – sizing him up.

'W . . . w . . . woodwolves,' he stammered.

The ruff of snow-white fur around their necks bristled at the sound of his voice. Twig swallowed. They were *whitecollar* woodwolves: the worst kind – and here was a whole pack of them. Twig inched back towards the air shaft. Too late. The woodwolves, noticing the movement, let out a low bloodcurdling growl. With open jaws and dripping fangs, the one nearest him leaped up from the ground and launched itself at his throat.

'Aaaargh!' Twig screamed. The outstretched paws of the beast thumped into his chest. The pair of them toppled backwards and landed heavily on the ground.

Twig kept his eyes shut tight. He could smell the warm rotten breath on his face as the wood-wolf sniffed and tasted. He felt a row of pinpricks along the side of his neck. The woodwolf had him in its jaws. One movement – from either of them – and that would be that.

Just then, above the deafening pounding of his heart, Twig heard a voice. 'What's going on here, then?' it said. 'What have you found, eh, lads? Something for the pot?'

The woodwolves snarled greedily, and Twig felt the teeth pressing down sharply into his skin.

'Drop it!' the voice commanded. 'Stealth! Drop it, I say!'

The teeth withdrew. The stench receded. Twig opened his eyes. A short elf-like creature clutching a heavy whip, was standing there and glaring at him. 'Friend or food?' he demanded.

'F . . . f . . . friend,' Twig stuttered.

'Get up, friend,' he said. The woodwolves twitched as Twig climbed to his feet. 'They won't hurt you,' he said, seeing Twig's discomfort. 'So long as I don't tell them to,' he smirked.

'You wouldn't do that,' said Twig. 'W . . . would you?'

'All depends,' came the reply. The woodwolves began pacing to and fro, licking their lips and yelping excitedly. 'We small people have to stay on our guard. Stranger equals danger, that's my motto. You can't be too careful in the Deepwoods.' He looked Twig up and down. 'Mind you,' he said, '*you* don't look too much of a threat.' He wiped his hand vigorously on his trousers and thrust it forward. 'The name's Garble,' he said. 'Garble the Hunter, and this here is my pack.' One of the wood-wolves snarled. Garble gave it a vicious kick.

Twig reached out and shook the hand being offered him. All round them, the woodwolves were whipping themselves up into a slavering frenzy. Garble stopped in mid-shake, pulled his hand away and inspected it.

'Blood,' he said. 'No wonder the lads found you. The smell of it drives them proper crazy, it does.' He crouched down and carefully wiped his hand on the grass until all trace of the blood had disappeared. He looked up. 'So what exactly are you?' he said.

'I'm . . .' Twig began, and then stopped. He wasn't a woodtroll. But then, what was he? 'I'm Twig,' he said simply.

'A twig? Never heard of 'em. You look a bit like a lop-ear or even a blunderhead. Even *I* find it difficult to tell them apart. Fetch a good price though, they do. The sky pirates are always after goblins from the wilder tribes. They make good fighters even if they are a bit difficult to control . . . Are the twigs good fighters?'

Twig shifted uneasily from foot to foot. 'Not really,' he said.

Garble sniffed. 'Wouldn't get much for you, anyway,' he said. 'Scrawny little specimen that you are. Still, you might make a ship's cook. Can you cook?'

'Not really,' Twig said again. He was inspecting his hand. There was a cut on his little finger, but it didn't look too bad.

'Just my luck,' said Garble. 'I was on the trail of a big lumpskull – would have made me a pretty penny, I can tell you – and what happens? He goes running straight into the jaws of a bloodoak and that's the end of him. Terrible mess. And then the boys pick up your scent. Hardly worth the bother,' he added, and spat on the ground.

It was then that Twig noticed what Garble the Hunter was wearing. The dark fur was unmistakeable. How many times had he stroked fur exactly like it: sleek, smooth and tinged with green.

'Banderbear,' Twig breathed, his blood beginning to boil. This obnoxious little elf was wearing the pelt of a banderbear.

Garble was shorter than Twig, considerably shorter. In a straight fight, Twig was sure he could overpower him easily. But, as the circle of yellow eyes stared at him unblinking, Twig had to swallow his indignation.

'Can't stand around all day, chatting,' Garble went on. 'I've got some serious hunting to be getting on with. Don't have time to waste on wolf-bait like you. I'd get that hand seen to, if I was you. Might not be so lucky next time. Come on, boys.'

And, with the yelping pack all round him, Garble

turned and disappeared into the trees.

Twig sank to his knees. He was back in the Deepwoods, but this time there was no banderbear to protect him. No sweet, lonely banderbear, just wolves and hunters and lumpskulls and blunderheads and . . .

'Why?' he wailed. 'Why all this? WHY?'

'Because,' came a voice – a voice that sounded gentle and kind.

Twig looked up and started with horror. The creature that had spoken looked neither gentle nor kind. In fact, she was monstrous.

'So what brings you . . . SLURP . . . to this part of the . . . SLURP . . . Deepwoods?' she said.

Twig kept his head down. 'I'm lost,' he said.

'Lost? Nonsense . . . SLURP . . . You're here!' she laughed.

Twig swallowed nervously. He raised his head.

'That's better . . . SLURP . . . Now why don't you tell me all about it, m'dear. Gabtrolls is very good . . . SLURP . . . listeners,' and she flapped her huge bat-like ears.

The yellow light of late afternoon glowed through the pink membrane of her ears, picking out the delicate network of blood vessels. It glistened on her greasy face and glinted on the eye-stalks. It was these – long, thick, rubbery, swaying; now contracting, now elongating, and both topped off with bulbous green spheres – which had so startled Twig. His stomach still felt queasy, yet he couldn't look away.

'Well?' the gabtroll said.

'I . . .' Twig began.

'SLURP!'

Twig shuddered. Each time the long yellow tongue flipped out to lick and moisten one or other of the unblinking green eyes, he forgot what he was going to say. The eye-stalks extended towards him. The eyeballs stared at both sides of his face at the same time. 'What you need, m'dear,' said the gabtroll finally, 'is a nice cup of . . . SLURP . . . oakapple tea. While we're waiting.'

As they walked side by side in the fading orange light, the gabtroll talked. And talked and talked and talked. And as she went on, in her soft lilting voice, Twig no longer noticed her ears or her eyes or even that long slurping tongue. 'I ain't never fitted in, you understand,' she was explaining.

Twig understood only too well.

'Course, gabtrolls have been purveyors of fruit and vegetables for generations,' she went on. 'Growing produce and selling it at the various market-clearings. Yet I knew . . .' She paused. 'I said to myself, Gabba, I said, you just b'ain't cut out for a life of hoeing and haggling. And that's a fact.'

They emerged in a glade bathed in the deep red glow of the setting sun. The light gleamed on something round and metallic. Twig squinted into the shadows. A small covered wagon was standing beneath the hanging fronds of a sallowdrop tree. The gabtroll waddled towards it. Twig watched as she unhooked a lantern and set it swinging from a branch.

'Throw a little light on the matter,' she chuckled, and proceeded to pull the wagon out from its hiding place.

Twig looked it over. For a moment, it seemed to disappear. He shook his head. It returned again.

'Clever, eh?' said the gabtroll. 'I spent ages mixing the paints.'

Twig nodded. From the wheels beneath the wooden frame to the animal skin which had been stretched over hoops to make a waterproof covering, every inch of the wagon had been daubed with various shades of green and brown. It was perfectly camouflaged for the forest. Twig's eyes focused on some writing on the side: curious curling letters that looked like twisted leaves.

'Yes, that's me,' said the gabtroll, with a lick of her eyeballs. '"Gabmora Gabtroll. Apothecaress and Wise One". Now let's see about that tea, shall we?'

She bustled up the wooden steps and disappeared inside the wagon. Twig watched her from the outside as she placed a kettle on the stove, and spooned some orange flakes into a pot.

'I'd ask you in . . .' she said, looking up. 'But, well . . .' She flapped her hand round at the chaos within the wagon.

There were stoppered jars and bottles swilling with amber liquid and the innards of small beasts, there were boxes and crates full of seeds and leaves, and sackfuls of nuts spilling onto the floor. There were tweezers and scalpels, and chunks of crystal, and a pair of scales, and sheaves of paper, and rolls of bark. Herbs and dried flowers hung in bunches from hooks, alongside strings of desiccated slugs, and a selection of dead animals: woodrats, oakvoles, weezits, all swaying gently as the gabtroll busied herself with the tea.

Twig waited patiently. The moon rose, and promptly vanished behind a bank of black cloud. The lamplight glowed brighter than ever. Beside a stubby log Twig noticed a heart shape had been scratched into the dirt. A stick lay across it.

'Here we are, m'dear,' said the gabtroll as she emerged, a steaming mug in each hand and a tin under her arm. She set everything down on the log. 'Help yourself to a seedrusk,' she said. 'I'll just get us something to park our behinds on.'

She unhooked two more of the logs from the underside of the wagon. Like everything else, they were so well camouflaged that Twig hadn't noticed them. She plonked herself down.

'But enough of me,' she said. 'I could go on for ever about my life in the Deepwoods, travelling from here to there, constantly on the move, mixing my potions and poultices and helping out wherever I can . . . How's the tea?'

Twig sipped and prepared to wince. 'It's . . . lovely,' he said, surprised.

'Oakapple peel,' she said. 'Good for the nails, good for the heart, and excellent for . . .' She coughed, and her eyes went in and out on their stalks. 'For keeping you *regular*, if you take my meaning. And taken with honey – as this is – it's an unbeatable cure for vertigo.' She leaned towards Twig and lowered her voice. 'Far be it for me to boast,' she said, 'but I know much more than most about the things which live and grow in the forest.'

Twig said nothing. He was thinking about the banderbear.

'I understand their *properties*,' she added, and sighed. 'For my pains.' She sipped her tea. Her eye-stalks looked round. One of them focused in on the stick lying across the heart shape. Take this for instance. What do you think it is?'

'A stick?'

'It's a heartcharmer,' she said. 'It shows me the path I have to follow.' She peered round into the forest. 'We still have time . . . Let me give you a little demonstration.'

She stood the stick in the centre of the heart with one finger holding it upright. She closed her eyes, whispered 'Heart lead me where you will', and lifted her finger. The stick dropped.

'But it's landed in exactly the same position as before,' said Twig.

'Naturally,' said the gabtroll. 'For that is the way my destiny leads.'

Twig jumped to his feet. He seized the stick. 'Can I have a go?' he said excitedly.

The gabtroll shook her head, and her eyes swung dole-

fully to and fro. 'You must find your own stick . . .'

Twig darted off towards the trees. The first one he came to was too high; the second too tough. The third was perfect. He climbed up and broke off a small branch, stripped the leaves and bark until it looked just right, and jumped down again.

'Aaaargh!' he screamed, as something – some ferocious, slavering black beast – seized him, slammed him to the ground and pinned him down. The silhouette of its massive shoulders flickered in the lamp-light. Its yellow eyes glinted. Its jaws opened and . . .

It yowled with pain.

'Karg!' the gabtroll screamed, as she brought the stick down on the beast's nose for a second time. 'How many times have I got to tell you? Only carrion! Now take your food and get to the wagon this instant. And hurry up about it. You're late!'

Reluctantly, the beast released Twig's shoulders. It turned, sunk its teeth into the corpse of a tilder lying next to the tree, and dragged it obediently back towards the glade.

The gabtroll helped Twig to his feet. 'Nothing damaged,' she said, looking him over. She nodded towards his attacker. 'A much underrated beast, the prowlgrin. Loyal – generally. Intelligent – very. And stronger than any ox. What's more, as its owner, you don't have to worry about food. It takes care of itself. If I could just get it to stick to animals that have already died.' Her eyes bounced about as she laughed. 'Can't have it eating my customers. Bad for business!'

Back at the clearing, the prowlgrin was crouched down between the shafts of the wagon, tearing into the remains of the dead tilder. The gabtroll slipped a harness over its head, tied a girth around its middle and fastened the straps.

Twig stood to one side, watching, stick in hand. 'You're not going, are you?' he said, as she slung the logs and tea things into the back of the wagon. 'I thought . . .'

'I was just waiting for Karg to get himself fed and watered,' she explained, climbing up into the front seat. She took up the reins. 'Now, I'm afraid . . . Places to go, people to heal . . .'

'But what about me?' said Twig.

'I *always* travel alone,' said the gabtroll firmly. She tugged on the reins and set off.

Twig watched the lamp swaying back and forth as the wagon clattered away. Before he was plunged once again into darkness, he stood his stick in the centre of the heart. His fingers trembled as he held it in place. He closed his eyes and whispered softly, 'Heart lead me where you will.' He lifted his finger. Opened his eyes. The stick was still standing.

He tried again. Finger on. 'Heart lead me . . .' Finger off. Still the stick did not fall.

'Hey!' Twig cried out. 'The stick's just standing there.' The gabtroll peered round the side of the wagon, her eye-stalks gleaming in the lamplight. 'Why won't it fall down?'

'Haven't a clue, m'dear,' she replied, and with that she was gone.

'Some wise one!' Twig muttered angrily, and kicked the stick far away into the undergrowth.

The flickering lamplight disappeared. Twig turned and stumbled off into the darkness in the opposite direction, cursing his luck. No-one stays. No-one cares. And it's all my fault. I should never, *ever* have strayed from the path.

CHAPTER TWELVE

The Sky Pirates

Far above Twig's head, the clouds thinned. They swirled and squirmed around the moon like a bucketful of maggots.

Twig stared upwards, spellbound, horrified: so much skybound activity while, down on the forest floor, it was all so still. Not a leaf stirred. The heavy air felt charged.

All at once, a flash of blue-white light splashed across the far reaches of the sky. Twig counted. When he got to eleven, a booming roll of thunder rumbled. Again the sky lit up, brighter than before; again the thunder sounded. This time Twig only counted to eight. The storm was getting closer.

He began to run. Slipping, stumbling, sometimes falling, he hurried across the treacherous forest floor – now bright as day, now black as pitch. A wind had got up, dry, electric. It tousled his hair and set the fleece of his hammelhornskin waistcoat bristling.

With his eyes full of the pinky after-dazzle of each lightning bolt, the darkness that followed was all the darker. Twig staggered on blindly. The wind gusted at his back. There was a crackle in the sky directly above his head and a jagged fork of absolute brilliance tore the sky apart. The thunder struck at once with a CR-R-R-R-R-R-ASH! The air trembled. The earth shook. Twig fell to the ground and wrapped his arms around his head. 'It's f . . . falling,' he stammered. 'The open sky is falling.'

A second eye-blinding ear-splitting mix of thunder and lightning battered the forest. Then a third. And a fourth. Yet all the time, that space between the two was growing. Twig climbed shakily to his feet. The forest, one moment brightly lit like a tribe of dancing skeletons, the next plunged into darkness, was still around him; the sky still above.

He climbed one of the trees, a tall and ancient lufwood to watch the storm receding. Up and up, he went. The swirling wind plucked at his hands and feet. At the top, he rested in a swaying fork, panting for breath. The air smelled of rain, but no rain fell. The lightning stabbed, the sky glowed, the thunder rumbled. Abruptly, the wind dropped.

Twig wiped his eyes and, with his fingers, combed away the last remaining beads and bows. He watched them bounce and flutter out of sight below him. He looked up, and there, just for a second, silhouetted against the lightning sky . . .

Twig's heart missed a beat. 'A sky ship,' he whispered.

The lightning faded. The ship disappeared. Another flash, and the sky lit up again.

'But now it's facing the other way,' Twig said. More lightning, and the sky grew brighter still. 'It's spinning,' he gasped. 'It's caught in a whirlwind.'

Round and round the sky ship went, faster and faster; so fast that even Twig felt dizzy. The mainsail flapped wildly; the rigging lashed the air. Powerless, out of control, the sky ship was being dragged towards the swirling vortex at the centre of the storm.

Suddenly, a single solitary finger of lightning zigzagged down out of the cloud. It hurtled towards the spinning sky ship – and struck. The ship rolled to one side. Something small and round and twinkling like a star fell away from the side, and tumbled down towards the forest below. The sky ship spiralled down after it.

Twig gasped. The sky ship was dropping out of the sky like a stone.

It went dark again. Twig chewed his hair, his scarf, his nails. It remained dark. 'One more flash,' Twig pleaded. 'Just so I can see what's . . .'

The flash came, illuminating a long stretch across the distant horizon. In the dim light, Twig saw three bat-like creatures hovering above the falling ship. And, as he watched, two . . . three more joined them, each one leaping from the decks and fluttering away on the ebbing

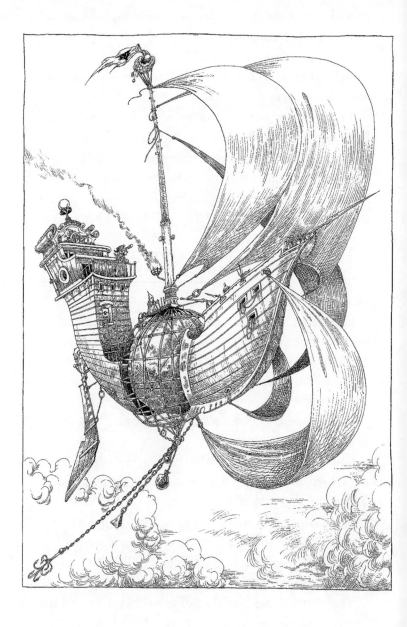

wind. The sky pirates were abandoning ship. An eighth figure leaped to safety just seconds before the sky ship crashed down into the forest canopy.

Twig flinched. Had the whole crew managed to escape in time? Had the sky ship been smashed to bits? Had the flying figures he'd seen landed safely?

He fairly flew back down the tree and raced off through the woods as fast as his legs would carry him. The moon was shining bright and clear, and the night animals were all in full voice. The trees, shot with their own shadows, looked as if they'd been draped in long nets. Apart from the occasional fallen branch, and whiff of smouldering greenwood, there was no sign that the storm had passed that way. Twig ran till he could run no more.

He stood doubled over, a stitch in his side, and gulped for breath. Moonbirds twittered loudly from their perches above his head. Then Twig heard another noise. A hissing. A spitting. He walked forwards. It seemed to be coming from a combbush just up ahead. He pushed the branches aside, and was immediately struck by a blast of intense heat.

Lying half-buried in the ground was a rock. It was enormous and round, and glowed white-hot. The grass around it had shrivelled, the overhanging bush was charred. Twig squinted at the rock, sheltering his eyes from the heat and dazzle. Could this be the *star* he'd seen falling from the sky ship. He looked round. The ship and its crew couldn't be far away.

The moonbirds were squawking irritably over something or other. Twig clapped his hands, and they flew off. Out of the silence that followed, Twig heard the low murmur of voices.

He crept forwards. The voices grew louder. He caught sight of a tall, heavy-set red-faced man with a thick knotted beard, and ducked down behind a fallen branch. It was a sky pirate.

'We'd best find the others,' he was saying, his voice deep and chewy. He chuckled. 'The look on Slyvo's face when he jumped. White as codflesh he was, and green at the gills.'

'He was up to something,' a reedy voice replied matter-of-factly. 'Up to no good.'

Twig stretched up to see who was speaking.

'You're not wrong there, Spiker,' said the bearded pirate gruffly. 'He's not been happy since that business with the ironwood. That 'lectric storm was a blessing in disguise, or my name's not Tem Barkwater.' He paused. 'I just hope the cap'n's all right.'

'Sky willing,' came the reply.

Twig stretched up again, but could still see only the one pirate. He stepped up onto the branch for a better look and – CRACK – the wood gave under his foot.

'What was that?' bellowed Tem Barkwater. He spun round and scoured the silvery shadows.

'Probably just an animal,' the second sky pirate said.

'I'm not so sure,' said Tem Barkwater slowly.

Twig cowered down. The whispering sound of tip-toe footsteps approached. Twig looked up. He found himself staring into the delicate yet broad face of someone little older than himself – an oakelf by the look of him. It must be Spiker.

The oakelf stared at Twig, a puzzled frown playing over his features. Finally, 'Do I know you?' he said.

'You find anything?' Tem Barkwater called.

Spiker continued to stare. His tufted ears twitched. 'Yes,' he said quietly.

'What's that?'

'I said *yes*!' he shouted back, and seized Twig by the shoulder. The hammelhornskin fleece turned at once to needles, and stabbed the oakelf's hand. He yelped, pulled away and sucked his fingers tenderly, all the while staring suspiciously at Twig. 'Follow me,' he instructed.

'What have we here, then?' said Tem Barkwater, as Spiker and Twig emerged before him. 'Lanky little so'n'so, ain't he?' he said, and squeezed Twig's upper arm with a bulging finger and thumb. 'Who are you, lad?'

'Twig, sir,' said Twig.

'Extra hand on board, eh?' he said, and winked at Spiker.

Twig felt a thrill of excitement shudder through his body.

'If there's still an "on board" left,' the oakelf commented.

'Course there is!' said Tem Barkwater. He laughed throatily. 'Just a matter of finding out where it's got to.'

Twig cleared his throat. 'I think it's over there,' he said, pointing to his right.

Tem Barkwater turned and stooped and pressed his large, red hairy face into Twig's. 'And how would you know that?'

'I . . . I saw it crash,' he said uncertainly.

'You *saw* it,' he bellowed.

'I was up a tree. Watching the storm. I saw the sky ship get trapped in the whirlwind.'

'You saw it,' Tem Barkwater repeated, more softly now. He clapped his hands together. 'Then you'd better lead us there, Twig, me-old-mucker.'

It was a mixture of luck and guesswork that got him there, but get there he did. They hadn't gone more than a hundred steps before Tem Barkwater spied the hull ahead of them, glinting in the moonlight high up in the branches. 'There she is,' he murmured. 'The *Stormchaser*, herself. Well done, lad,' he said to Twig, and slapped him heartily on the shoulder.

'Sssh!' hissed Spiker. 'We're not the first ones back.'

Tem cocked his head to one side. 'It's that rogue of a quartermaster, Slyvo Spleethe,' he muttered.

Spiker raised a finger to his lips, and the three of them stood stock-still, straining to hear the murmured conversation.

'It would seem, my dear Mugbutt, that our captain has over-reached himself,' Slyvo was saying. His voice was nasal and precise, with every *d* and *t* being spat out like something distasteful.

'Over-reached himself!' came a low gruff echo.

Tem Barkwater shifted about restlessly. His face grew thunderously dark. He craned his neck. 'The Stone Pilot's with them, too,' he whispered.

Twig stole a glance through a gap in the leaves. There were three pirates there. Mugbutt was a flat-head goblin. With his broad flat skull and wide ears, he was typical of his kind, yet fiercer by far than the flat-head who had helped Twig out of the swamp. Behind him stood a squat creature dressed in a heavy overcoat and heavier boots.

His head was hidden beneath a large pointed hood which extended down over his chest. Two round glass panels allowed him to see out. He did not speak. The third pirate was Slyvo Spleethe himself; a tall yet stooped figure, all angles and points. His nose was long, his chin sharp, and behind his steel-rimmed spectacles his shifty eyes were constantly on the move.

'I mean, far be it from me to say I told you so,' he continued, 'but . . . well . . . If we *had* left the ironwood, *as* I suggested . . . The price of the stuff is plummeting anyway at the moment.' There was a pause, and a sigh. 'If we *had* left it, we wouldn't have been anywhere near the storm.'

'Near the storm,' growled Mugbutt.

'Still. Who am *I* to argue with fate? If the command of the ship was destined to fall upon my shoulders, I must accept my responsibility with . . .' He searched for the right word.

Mugbutt filled the silence. 'Responsibility with . . .'

'Oh, do stop interrupting me!' Slyvo snapped. 'You are brave in battle, Mugbutt, don't get me wrong; a credit to your tribe. But you lack any sense of occasion.'

'Occasion,' Mugbutt repeated.

Slyvo grunted impatiently. 'Come,' he said. 'Let's break the glad tidings to the others.'

Tem could remain still no longer. 'Treacherous dog,' he growled as he burst through the undergrowth and into the clearing. The Stone Pilot, Mugbutt and Slyvo Spleethe all spun round.

'My *dear* Tem,' said Slyvo, his disappointment turning

instantly to a tight-lipped smile. 'And Spiker. You two made it too.'

Twig held back; watching, listening.

'*He* ought to be chained up,' said Tem, pointing at the flat-head goblin. 'Cap'n's orders.'

Slyvo lowered his head coyly and fiddled with one of the knots in his moustache. 'The thing is,' he whimpered, looking up over his glasses. 'As I was just saying to Mugbutt here, our illustrious captain, Quintinius Verginix, is . . .' He looked round theatrically. '*Not* here.' He smirked. 'And Mugbutt does *so* enjoy his freedom.'

Tem grunted. For the time being, at least, there was nothing he could do. 'What state is the ship in?' he asked.

Slyvo looked up. 'How's it going, Stope?' he called.

'OK,' came a voice, which squeaked as it spoke. 'Superficial damage, mainly. The rudder's taken a hammering. But nothing I can't fix.'

'Will she soon be sky-worthy?' said Slyvo impatiently.

A head poked out from the overhead foliage. A hard bullet-head it was, with a close-fitting metal frame over the skull which held a bolted jaw in place. 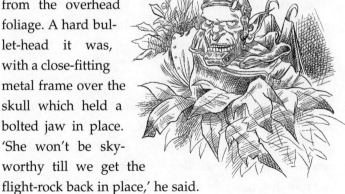 'She won't be sky-worthy till we get the flight-rock back in place,' he said.

Slyvo grimaced and stamped his feet sulkily. 'Can't you improvise? Lufwood, bloodoak – they rise. Just burn more . . .'

Stope Boltjaw tutted and shook his head. 'Can't do it,' he said. 'You could never contain a fire the size it would have to be to achieve the required lift, and besides . . .'

'There must be *something* you can do!' Slyvo screamed. 'I still don't understand why the blasted rock fell in the first place.'

'Coz it was struck by lightning,' said Stope Boltjaw.

'I know *that*, you idiot!' snapped Slyvo. 'But . . .'

'Cold rock rises, hot rock sinks,' Stope continued patiently. 'Scientific fact. And I'll tell you another scientific fact. What heats up, cools down. If you lot don't find that flight-rock before much longer, it'll have floated off for ever. And now, if you'll excuse me, I've got the cradle-moorings to repair – just in case you should find it.' His head disappeared back behind the leafy branches.

Slyvo bit into his lips. The blood drained from his face. 'You heard him,' he snarled. 'FIND THE FLIGHT-ROCK!'

Spiker and Mugbutt turned and hurried off. The Stone Pilot plodded after them. Tem Barkwater held his ground.

'Well?' Slyvo demanded.

'I might be able to tell you where the rock is. On one condition. When it's back in place, we wait for the cap'n.'

'Oh, but of *course*,' said Slyvo. 'I give you my *word*.' He reached out and shook Tem by the hand.

From his place in the undergrowth, Twig saw the

quartermaster's other arm swing round behind his back. The hand was missing two fingers, and the raw scars looked recent. The two remaining fingers were stiffly crossed.

Tem nodded. 'I aim to ensure that you keep your word,' he said. He turned away. 'Twig,' he called out. 'Are you there, lad? Come out where I can see you.'

Twig stood up and stepped forwards.

'A spy!' hissed Slyvo.

'A witness,' said Tem. 'To what you promised.' He turned to Twig. 'Do you know where the flight-rock landed?' he asked. Twig hesitated. He glanced up at Slyvo Spleethe. 'It's all right,' Tem assured him.

Twig nodded. 'I know, all right,' he admitted. 'I saw it. Like a shooting star it looked – well, a *dropping* star. A *falling* star . . .'

'Get on with it!' said Slyvo sharply.

Twig blushed. He was talking too much. But he couldn't help it. The whiff of adventure about the rough and rugged sky pirates quickened his heart and loosened his tongue. He turned away from Slyvo's intense gaze and started walking. 'It's this way,' he said.

'Hey, you lot,' Slyvo Spleethe called out to Spiker, Mugbutt and the Stone Pilot. 'Follow us.'

Twig led the ragtag rabble of pirates back through the forest. The way looked familiar in the swaying lamp-light. He first heard, and then saw the humming combbush. He marched up to it and parted the branches. The stone was still there, embedded in the ground. It glowed a deep buttery yellow.

'It was white before,' said Twig.

'It's cooling down,' said Tem. 'The trick will be to get it back to the sky ship while it's light enough to carry, but heavy enough not to fly away.'

Slyvo turned to the Stone Pilot. '*You* are responsible for transporting it,' he said.

From deep within the Stone Pilot's pointed hood came a grunt of acknowledgement. He lumbered forwards, crouched down and embraced the rock in his broad arms. The sleeves and front of his fireproof coat hissed. Twig sniffed. The air smelt of scorched mud. The Stone Pilot heaved and strained, and the glass panels at the front of his hood misted over. But the flight-rock did not budge.

'Empty your water flasks onto it,' said Tem.

'Yes,' Slyvo said, remembering his new responsibilities. 'Empty your water flasks onto it.' He and the others began pouring water onto the glowing stone. Where it landed, the water hissed and turned the rock a shade of orange. 'More!' Slyvo commanded.

The sky pirates trotted off, returning soon after with their flasks refilled. Little by little, the rock turned a rich deep red. It began to wobble in its earthy setting. The Stone Pilot tried again. This time the rock came out of the ground with a soft *ssss-quap*.

Staggering under the weight and wheezing, the Stone Pilot trudged back to the clearing. The others tramped after him. Because of the intense heat radiating from the rock, there was nothing they could do to help, nothing but hope and pray.

The hull of the sky ship came into view. 'We've got it, Stope,' Tem called ahead. 'We've got the flight-rock.'

'I'll be ready directly,' Stope Boltjaw shouted back, and Twig again noticed the squeaking sound as he spoke. 'I'm just making sure the grappling hooks and anchor are secure,' he said. 'Wouldn't want her leaving without us.'

The Stone Pilot grumbled. The cooling rock was threatening to slip out of his grasp at any moment.

'Have you rigged up the cradle?' Slyvo called up.

'What do you take me for?' came the irritated reply. 'Of course I have! I used some of the ironwood. It's less buoyant than lufwood or bloodoak, but more fire-resistant – in case the rock's still too hot.'

The Stone Pilot grunted urgently.

'It's rising!' Spiker yelled.

Stope Boltjaw's head appeared out of the tree. 'Can you climb with it?' he asked.

The Stone Pilot shook his head and groaned. It was all he could do to keep the increasingly buoyant rock in his grasp.

'In that case,' Stope called down. 'We'll go for plan B. But it'll need pinpoint accuracy if it's going to work. The Stone Pilot will have to get the rock *directly* beneath the cradle before releasing it. So, left a couple of paces . . .'

The Stone Pilot shuffled awkwardly to the left.

'Stop. Forwards a tad. STOP! Back a bit. Left. Back a bit more.' Stope paused. 'That should do it,' he whispered. 'When I say *now*, let the rock go – but be careful not to nudge it when you do.'

Twig peered up into the tree. He saw Stope Boltjaw open the door of a cage-like contraption attached to the centre of the hull. He held it open with his foot and raised a long harpoon ready.

'Now!' he called.

The Stone Pilot gently released his load. For a moment, the rock hovered in the air. It rotated. Then it began to rise, slowly at first, but soon gathering speed. Twig saw Stope Boltjaw bracing himself against a branch. The rock came closer. It was going to miss the cradle! Stope leaned forwards and gently prodded the rock with his harpoon. It shifted slightly to the left, and continued rising.

'Come on, come on,' Slyvo urged the flying rock. He turned to Mugbutt. 'If he does it, I want everyone on board at once,' he hissed. Twig listened closely. 'And if Tem Barkwater objects,' he went on, 'deal with him, Mugbutt. OK?'

KER-DONK! The stone landed in the cradle. SLAM-CLICK. Stope Boltjaw kicked the door shut with his foot. He bent down and secured the catch. 'Done it!' he roared triumphantly.

Twig's heart fluttered. The wonderful pirate ship was sky-worthy once more, and he whooped and cheered with the rest.

'This shall not go unremembered, Stope Boltjaw,' Slyvo announced. 'Well done!'

'Yes!' came a second voice, deep and sonorous. 'Well done!'

Everyone spun round.

'Cap'n!' Tem Barkwater grinned. 'You made it!'

'Indeed I did, Tem,' came the solemn reply.

Twig gazed at the captain. He looked magnificent. He was tall and, unlike the stooping Slyvo Spleethe, stood upright, proud and elegant. His side whiskers were waxed, and a black

leather patch stretched across one eye. From his long pirate's coat hung a multitude of objects: from goggles and telescope to grappling irons and daggers. By his side was a long curved cutlass, which glinted in the silver moonlight. Twig started. Hadn't he seen such a cutlass before, with its jewelled handle and nick in the blade?

Just then, an eighth figure emerged from the undergrowth. Twig stared. It was a banderbear, though quite different from his old friend, for this one was white with red eyes – an albino. It pulled the dead body of a hammelhorn from its shoulder and let it fall to the ground. Then it took its place behind the captain.

'Ah, Hubble,' the captain said. 'Just who I wanted to see. Take the flat-head and chain him up.'

The banderbear pointed up to the sky ship. 'Wuh?' it said.

'No,' said the captain. 'To a tree. But a strong one, mind.'

Mugbutt snarled and raised a fist in defiance. The banderbear swatted it

away and seized the chain round the goblin's neck, almost lifting him off his feet.

'Easy, Hubble,' ordered the captain.

The banderbear lowered its arm and jerked the chain. Mugbutt was led away.

'Do you think that is altogether *wise*, sire?' came the whining voice of Slyvo Spleethe. 'Here we are in the Deepwoods. *Anything* might be out there ... Mugbutt could be useful in case of a surprise attack.'

The captain turned and fixed Slyvo with his good eye. 'Do you think I cannot read your mutinous heart, Spleethe?' he said. 'Your friends in the Undertown League of Free Merchants are no use to you out here in the Deepwoods. We're an independent crew, and *I* give the orders. One more word and I'll have you sky-fired. Do I make myself clear?'

'What's sky-fired?' Twig whispered to Spiker.

'Tied to a branch of burning bloodoak,' the oakelf whispered back. 'You go up like a rocket, screaming all the way.'

Twig shuddered.

'We'll stay here the night and depart at first light,' the captain was saying. He turned to Tem. 'Right then, ship's cook,' he said, kicking at the dead hammelhorn. 'Get cooking!'

'Aye-aye, cap'n,' said Tem keenly.

'Spiker, plot us a route back to Undertown. I don't want to be stuck in these accursèd woods any longer than necessary.' He looked up. 'How much longer will you need to effect repairs, Boltjaw?'

'A couple of hours, cap'n,' came the reply. 'I've just got to chamfer the new bidgits and realign the rudder pins . . .'

'And the Stone Pilot?'

'He's down in the engine room re-boring the flange ducts.'

'Excellent work,' said the captain. He turned and looked down at Twig.

And it was at that moment that Twig knew for sure that he had met the captain before. It was the eye-patch which had stopped him recognizing him at once. He was the one Tuntum and he had met all that time ago in the forest when his woodtroll father had been trying to set him up with a job. The tall elegant sky pirate with his jewelled sword – with the nick in the blade. How could he have forgotten?

'Why are you just standing there gawping?' the captain barked. 'Help the others with the fire.'

Twig set to work at once. He dashed into the forest to collect kindling. When he returned, however, the fire was already ablaze, roaring and crackling. With every log that Spiker and Tem Barkwater tossed onto the fire, a mighty shower of orange sparks filled the air. The fire sang and groaned and hissed with the different woods. Occasionally a piece of blazing lufwood floated up from the flames and soared off into the sky like an emergency flare.

Twig shuddered. Growing up with the woodtrolls, he had been taught to respect fire – the most treacherous necessity of all to a forest-dweller. That was why they burnt buoyant woods in stoves. The sky pirates' carelessness appalled him.

He was busy kicking burning branches back into the main blaze when Hubble returned from chaining Mugbutt securely to the tree. It was looking for the captain, yet as it passed Twig, it paused.

'Wuh!' it bellowed, and pointed at the tooth around Twig's neck.

'I wouldn't go too near Hubble if I was you,' Tem Barkwater called. 'It's an unpredictable beast at the best of times.'

But Twig took no notice. Despite the white bander-bear's ferocious appearance, there was a familiar sadness in its eyes. It stretched out a claw and gently touched the tooth.

'T-wuh-g,' it growled.

Twig stared back in amazement. Hubble knew who he was. He remembered the times his old friend had yodelled to the moonlit sky. He remembered the yodelled replies. Could it have been Hubble's desolate cry that Twig had heard the night the banderbear had died?

Hubble touched its chest and then pointed to Twig. 'Fr-uh-nz,' it said.

Twig smiled. 'Friends,' he said.

At that moment, there came the sound of the captain's angry voice. He wanted Hubble, and he wanted him now. Hubble swung round and plodded off obediently. Twig looked up to see Tem Barkwater staring at him in disbelief.

'I swear I have never seen the like in all my born days,'

he said. 'Friends with a banderbear! Whatever next?' He shook his head. 'Come on, young'un,' he said. 'Help me over here.'

Tem was standing by the fire. Having expertly skinned the hammelhorn, he had skewered it on a length of ironwood and placed it above the flames. The air was now thick with the smell of roasting meat. Twig joined him, and the pair of them turned the spit round and round, round and round.

By the time that Stope Boltjaw announced he had finished his repairs and came down from the tree, the hammelhorn was cooked. Tem banged a gong.

'Grub's up!' he called.

Twig sat down between Tem Barkwater and Spiker. The captain and Hubble were opposite them, with Slyvo Spleethe sitting back a little, in the shadows. The Stone Pilot hadn't appeared, and Mugbutt the flat-head goblin, still chained to a tree, had to make do with the scraps he was thrown.

As the sky pirates filled their empty stomachs with black bread and steaming chunks of hammelhorn meat, washed down with mugfuls of woodale, their spirits lifted.

'Of course,' laughed Tem Barkwater, 'we've been in worse scrapes than this, ain't we, cap'n?'

The captain grunted. He didn't seem to feel like talking.

'Why, that time we raided the league ships over Sanctaphrax itself. Never thought we'd get away with it. Cornered we were, nowhere to run, and a boarding party of wild flat-head goblins with murder on their minds popping up out of the cargo holds of those big, fat league ships. Never seen Spleethe shake so much – nor run so fast, neither. Kept saying, "There should have been liverbirch in the holds!" . . .'

'And so there should,' muttered Slyvo. 'Would have made us all a packet, too . . .'

'But the captain wasn't running, oh no, not him – not Cloud Wolf,' Tem chuckled. 'He just pulled out that great sword of his and set about the lot of them, Hubble following on behind. It was murder all right, but not the kind those goblins had in mind. That's where we got Mugbutt. Only one left standing. Mighty good fighter, but needs watching . . . It's also where the captain lost 'is eye. Fair exchange, he calls it.'

'Enough, Tem,' sighed the captain.

'It weren't no fair exchange when I lost my jaw,' broke in Stope Boltjaw, his ironwood replacement squeaking as he spoke. 'Had my back turned attending to the grappling socket. Ulbus Pentephraxis creeps up behind me with a hunting axe. I never stood a chance.' He spat into the fire. '*He's* now a league captain living the life of luxury in Undertown. Leaguesmen!' He hawked and spat again.

'Oh, they're not so bad,' wheedled Slyvo Spleethe, shifting closer to the fire. 'Now when *I* was starting out in Undertown as . . .'

'Spiker,' the captain interrupted. 'Have you plotted that course?' The oakelf nodded. 'Good lad,' he said, and looked slowly round the circle of pirates, suddenly sombre. 'The three rules of sky sailing. Never set sail before you've plotted your course, never fly higher than your longest grappling rope, and on no account dock in uncharted areas.'

The pirates nodded earnestly. Each and every one of them knew the perils of getting lost in the vast green leafy ocean. The fire was low. Twig watched the flickering flames reflected in the captain's thoughtful eye.

'I did that once,' he went on. 'Landed where I should not have landed.' He sighed. 'But then I had no choice.'

The pirates looked at one another in surprise. It was unlike the captain to speak of himself. They topped up their mugs and drew closer. The darkness wrapped itself around them.

'A wet and stormy night, it was,' Captain Quintinius Verginix – Cloud Wolf – began. Twig's body tingled with excitement. 'A cold night,' he said. 'A night of expectation and of sorrow.'

Twig hung on his every word.

'At that time I was a crew member on board a league ship.' He looked round at the circle of faces, bathed in the dying fire-glow, mouths open, eyes wide, and smiled. 'You load of ruffians,' he chuckled. 'If you think I'm a hard taskmaster, you should have served under Multinius Gobtrax. Ruthless, demanding, punctilious – the worst sort of league captain you'll ever meet.'

Twig watched the fireflies playing roly-poly in the air and darting in and out of the leaves. The wind had dropped completely and his hair and skin felt damp. He chewed on the corner of his scarf.

'Picture it,' the captain said. Twig closed his eyes. 'There were but five of us on board the ship, and only four who were in any state to sail her: Gobtrax and his bodyguard, the Stone Pilot and me. Maris was already nine months with child. The storm had caught us unawares and dragged us way off course. Worse than that, the up-currents were terrible strong. Before we could weigh anchor or secure the grappling irons, we'd been sucked up, far above the forest and towards ... open sky.'

Twig's head spun. Straying from the path was bad enough, but being lost in open sky . . .

'We lowered the sails, but still we continued to rise. I crouched down next to Maris. "Everything's going to be all right," I said, though I scarce believed it myself. We would never get back to Undertown before she went into labour, and even if we did – the birth of the child was little cause for celebration.'

Twig opened his eyes and looked at the captain. He was staring into the glowing embers of the fire, playing idly with the waxed points of his side-whiskers. His single eye shone moistly.

'Was there something wrong with it?' asked Twig.

The captain stirred. 'No,' he said. 'Only the fact that it was a child at all . . .' He paused, and his eye glazed over. 'Maris and I had big decisions to make,' he said. 'I was ambitious. I intended one day to command my own sky ship – I couldn't be doing with a child weighing me down. A captain or a father, that was the choice I had. It was no choice at all. I told Maris that we could travel together, but *she* would have to choose between the baby and me. She chose me.' He breathed deeply in, and out. 'Mother Horsefeather agreed to take the child off our hands.'

Complete silence fell around the camp-fire. The pirates looked down at the ground awkwardly. They felt uneasy listening to their Cloud Wolf opening up in this way. Tem Barkwater busied himself with stoking up the fire.

The captain sighed. 'At least, that was the plan. Yet

there we were, miles from Undertown, and being drawn ever upwards.' He nodded up to the sky ship. 'It was the Stone Pilot who saved us then, as he saved us this evening. He doused the buoyant-wood burners, released the balance-weights, and when that was not enough, he climbed over the side and began chipping away at the flight-rock. Bit by bit, as slivers and shards broke off, our ascent slowed. Then we stopped. Then we started to go down. By the time the hull of the ship touched down on the forest, there were six on board. Maris had given birth.'

The captain stood up and began pacing agitatedly back and forth. 'What to do?' he said. 'We were grounded now in the Deepwoods, and the baby wouldn't survive the journey on foot back to Undertown. Gobtrax ordered us to get rid of the brat. He said he wouldn't wait. Maris was hysterical, but Gobtrax's bodyguard – a hulking great cloddertrog – made it clear that he'd snap my neck if I objected ... What *could* I do?'

The pirates shook their heads earnestly, solemnly. Tem poked at the fire.

'We left the sky ship and set off into the forest. I remember how loud the creatures of the night were, and how still the tiny bundle in Maris's arms. Then we came across a small village of woodtrolls ...'

Twig started. The hairs at the back of his neck stood on end. Icy shivers strummed his spine.

'Odd creatures,' the captain mused. 'Stocky, dark, not that bright. They live in tree cabins ... I had to tear the child away from Maris. The look in her eyes at that moment! It was as if all the life drained out of her. She never spoke a word again . . .' The captain sniffed.

Twig's heart beat faster and faster.

'I wrapped the baby up in a shawl,' he went on, his voice little more than a whisper. 'The birthing-shawl that Maris had made for it. Stitched it all herself, she did. With a lullabee tree for luck, she said. I left the bundle at the foot of a cabin tree, and the pair of us left. We didn't once look back.'

The captain paused and stared ahead into the shadows of the forest, hands clasped behind his back. Despite the roaring flames, Twig was cold. He had to clamp his jaws firmly shut to still his chattering teeth.

'You made the right decision, cap'n,' said Tem Barkwater quietly.

The captain turned. 'I made the *only* decision, Tem,' he replied. 'It's in the blood. My father was a sky pirate captain, as was his father, and his father before him. Perhaps . . .'

Twig's head was whirling, buzzing; thought after thought collided with one another. The abandoned baby. The woodtrolls. The scarf – his comfort cloth, still tightly tied around his neck. *My* scarf, he thought. He stared at the majestic sky pirate captain. Could you really be my father? he wondered. Does your blood flow through my veins? Will I also command a sky ship one day?

Maybe. Maybe not. There was something Twig had to know. 'Th . . . the baby,' he said nervously.

The captain spun round and looked at him, actually seeing him it seemed for the first time. The eyebrow above the patch raised questioningly.

'This is Twig, cap'n,' said Tem Barkwater. 'He found the flight-rock and . . .'

'I believe the lad can speak for himself,' said the captain. 'What did you want to say?'

Twig climbed to his feet and looked down at the ground. His breath came short and jerky; he could barely speak. 'Sire,' he said. 'Was the baby a g . . . girl . . . – or a boy?'

Quintinius Verginix stared back at Twig, his brow deeply furrowed. Perhaps he could not remember. Perhaps he remembered only too well. He stroked his chin. 'It was a boy,' he said finally. The sound of chains jangled behind him as Mugbutt rolled over in his sleep. The captain drained his mug and wiped his mouth. 'Early start tomorrow,' he said. 'We could all do with some shut-eye.'

Twig thought he would never sleep again. His heart was a-flutter, his imagination was working overtime.

'Hubble, you're on first watch,' the captain said. 'Wake me at four.'

'Wuh,' the banderbear grunted.

'And be careful of our treacherous friend here.'

Twig started with alarm, until he realized the captain was referring to Slyvo Spleethe.

'Here,' said Spiker, as he handed Twig a blanket. 'Take this. I'll be warm enough tonight in my caternest.' And with that, the oakelf climbed the tree, boarded the sky ship and made his way up to the cocoon at the top of the mast.

Twig wrapped the blanket around him and lay down on a bed of quilted leaf-fall. The fire was burning bright and hot. Glittering sparks and glowing embers rose skywards. Twig stared into the dancing flames.

But for the sky pirate – this captain Cloud Wolf, the one who had caused Spelda and Tuntum to send Twig away for fear he would be forced to join his crew – but for him, Twig would never have left the woodtroll village in the first place. He would never have strayed from the path. He would never have been lost.

But now he understood. He had *always* been lost, not just when he left the path but from the very beginning, when this sky pirate had left him wrapped in the birthing-shawl beneath the Snatchwood cabin. Now he'd been found again. Three short sentences kept going round and round his head.

I've found my path. I've found my destiny. I've found my father!

Twig closed his eyes. The image of the heartcharming stick pointing upwards sprang into his mind. That was where his future lay: in the sky, with his father.

CHAPTER THIRTEEN

THE GLOAMGLOZER

There was stillness. Then there was movement. Then there was stillness again.

The first stillness was that point of deepest, darkest silence shortly before the dawn. Twig rolled over, pulling Spiker's blanket tightly round him. His dreams were full of sky ships sailing across the indigo depths. Twig was standing at the helm. He raised his collar against the wind. 'Gallantly sailing,' he murmured, and smiled in his sleep.

The movement was brief and purposeful: a flurry of activity. Twig was still at the helm holding a straight course, while all around him the crew busied themselves with the nets as they flew towards an incoming flock of migrating snowbirds. It would be baked snowbird for supper.

The ropes clacked and jingled against the mast. 'Hard

to starboard,' came a voice. Twig sighed, and rolled over onto his other side.

The second stillness was orange – a desert of flickering emptiness. There were no more voices, not even his own. His back was cold, his face was hot. His eyes snapped open.

At first, what he saw made no sense. A fire in front of him. Charred bones and patches of grease in the dust. The dense canopy above, with stripes of bright early morning sunlight lancing the air.

Twig sat bolt upright. Suddenly, the events of the previous night came back to him. The storm. The sky ship. Stumbling across the flight-rock. Eating with the sky pirates. Finding his father ... So where were they all now?

They had gone without him. Twig howled with pain and loss and desolation. Tears streamed down his face, turning the stripy sunlight to star-shaped rainbows. They had left him behind! His choking sobs filled the air. 'Why, my father, why?' he cried out. 'Why have you abandoned me? Again!'

His words faded away, and with them his hopes of ever finding his way beyond the Deepwoods. He hung his head. The forest seemed quieter than usual. No coughing fromps, no squealing quarms, no screeching razorflits. Not only had the sky pirates gone, but it was as if they had taken all the woodland creatures with them.

Yet the air was not completely silent. There was a low roaring sound, a hissing sound, a crackling sound

which, even as Twig sat there with his head in his hands, grew in volume. The heat at his back became more intense. The hammelhornskin waistcoat began to prickle ominously. Twig spun round.

'Yaaaiii!' he screamed. It wasn't sunlight he had seen. It was fire. The Deepwoods were ablaze.

A piece of burning oakwood which had floated away from the sky pirates' slapdash fire had become lodged in the branches of a lullabee tree. The lullabee had smouldered and smoked; hours later it burst into flames. Fanned on by the stiff breeze, the fire had rapidly spread. Now, from the forest floor to the tips of the canopy leaves, a solid wall of red and orange flames was advancing across the forest.

The heat was overwhelming. Twig swooned as he stumbled to his feet. A blazing branch crashed down beside him, the sparks exploding like droplets of gold. Twig took to his heels and ran.

And he ran and he ran – with the wind at his side – trying desperately to reach the end of the fiery wall before the flames consumed him. He ran as he had never run before, yet not fast enough. At both ends, the wall of fire was curling round. Soon, he would be surrounded.

The burning air scorched the fur on his jacket, sweat poured over his face and streamed down his back, his head throbbed with the relentless blast of molten air. The curving ends of the wall closed in further.

'Faster,' Twig said, urging himself on. 'FASTER!'

He sped past a halitoad, whose short stubby front legs had slowed its escape, fatally. A hover worm, bewildered by the heat and smoke, flew round and round in circles before disappearing into the flames in an explosion of fetid steam. To his right, Twig caught sight of the writhing green of a tarry-vine trying in vain to dodge the advancing fire: the bloodoak it was attached to screamed and squalled as the first of the orange tongues lapped at the base of its trunk.

On and on Twig ran. The two ends of the wall of fire had almost come together now. He was all but encircled. His only hope of escape lay in the narrow gap remaining between the towering flames. Like two curtains hooked to the sky, they were being drawn across. Twig made a dash for the opening. His lungs burned with heat and acrid smoke; his head swam. As if in a dream, he watched the shimmering curtains of fire close.

Twig stopped and looked about him. He was slapbang in the middle of the burning circle. He was done for.

All round him, bushes and branches were smoking. Flames broke out, guttered and burst into life once again. Giant woodsucculents hissed and steamed as the water within their fat angular limbs began to boil. Fatter and fatter they grew, until – BANG, BANG, BA-BA-BA-BANG – they exploded. Like corks from bottles of woodfizz, their seeds shot through the air in a jet of frothing liquid.

The water doused the flames. But only for a second. Twig backed away from the advancing fire. He looked over his shoulder. It was getting closer there, too. To his left, to his right, the fire was closing in. Twig looked up

into the sky. 'Oh, Gloamglozer,' he whispered. 'Help.'

All at once, a tremendous noise cut through the roar of the fire. Twig spun round. The purple flames of a burning lufwood tree were dancing not twenty yards away. The creaking, cracking noise came again. Twig saw the whole tree tremble. It was about to fall on top of him. He glanced this way, that way. There was nowhere to run, nowhere to hide, and nothing to protect himself with. Again the noise echoed round about him – rasping, jarring, like the rotten tooth Twig had pulled from the banderbear's swollen jaw.

'NO!' Twig screamed as the tree wobbled and shook. For a second it remained suspended in the air. Twig fell to the ground and rolled into a ball. A blast of blistering air battered his body. He clamped his eyes shut and waited, petrified, for the tree to come crashing down on him.

Nothing happened. He waited some more. Still nothing. But how? Why? Twig lifted his head, opened his eyes – and gasped in amazement.

The massive lufwood tree – now a blazing purple inferno – was hovering above the ground. The wood, so buoyant when alight, had dragged the very roots from the earth and was rising slowly up towards the sky. On either side were two more lufwoods whose anchoring roots were, even now, being torn out of the ground. The melancholy voice of a lullabee filled the air as it, too, rose up above the blazing forest. The sky itself seemed to be on fire.

Where the burning trees had been, now there was darkness. It looked like a gappy smile. Twig seized his chance and made a headlong dash towards the sudden opening. He had to get there before it closed again.

'Near-ly . . . near-ly . . .' he panted.

The fire was on both sides of him. He ducked his head and lifted the collar of his jacket against the shimmering heat as he ran the gauntlet of flames. Just a few steps more . . . Just a little bit further . . .

He raised his arm to shield his eyes, and sprinted through the enclosing flames. His throat stung, his skin prickled, his nostrils caught the whiff of his own scorched hair.

All at once, the heat grew less intense. Twig was outside the circle of fire. He ran on a little more. The wind had dropped; the smoke was thickening. He stopped and turned and watched for a moment, as the great balls of purple and turquoise rose, ablaze and airborne, majestically into the darkening sky.

He'd done it. He'd escaped the forest fire!

Yet there was no time for congratulating himself. Not yet, at least. The coils of smoke were winding themselves around him; filling his eyes and mouth. Blinding him. Choking him.

On and on, Twig stumbled, breathing through his scarf which he held tightly against his face. Further and further. His head throbbed, his lungs ached, his eyes smarted and streamed. 'I can't go on,' Twig spluttered. 'I *must* go on.'

He kept walking till the roaring of the forest fire was just a memory, till the acrid smoke was replaced with a cold grey mist which – though as blindingly thick as the smoke – was wonderfully refreshing; he kept on to the very edge of the Deepwoods. And still he did not stop.

The mist thickened and thinned.

There were no more trees. No bushes, no shrubs, no plants or flowers. Beneath Twig's feet, the ground became hard, as the spongy earth of the Deepwoods gave way to a pavement of pitted rock, slippery from the thick greasy mist. He picked his way carefully over the treacherous slabs. One slip, and his foot would become wedged in the deep fissures between.

The mist thinned and thickened, as it always did. For these were the Edgelands, that narrow stretch of barren rock which separated the Deepwoods from the Edge itself. Beyond lay the unknown, the uncharted, the un-

explored; a place of seething craters and swirling fogs – a place into which even the sky pirates never ventured intentionally.

The gathering breeze blew in from over the Edge. It brought with it the whiff of sulphur as broad tongues of fog lolled over the top of the cliff and lapped at the rock. The air was filled with the moans and groans of an eternity of mournful lost souls. Or was it only the rising wind softly howling?

Twig trembled. Was this the place the caterbird had meant when he told him his destiny lay beyond the Deepwoods? He wiped the beads of water away from his face and leaped over a wide crack in the rock. As he landed, his ankle buckled under him. He yelped, collapsed and rubbed at the throbbing joint tenderly. Gradually, the pain grew less acute. He hobbled to his feet and tentatively placed his weight down.

'I think it's all right,' he muttered with relief.

Out of the sulphurous mist came a reply. 'I am glad to hear it, Master Twig,' it said.

Twig gasped. This was definitely not the wind playing tricks. It was a voice. A real voice. More than that, it was a *familiar* voice.

'You have travelled far since you strayed from the woodtroll path,' it continued, lilting, slightly mocking. 'So very, very far. And I have tracked you every step of the way.'

'Wh . . . who are you?' stammered Twig, peering into the grey swirling mists. 'Why can't I see you?'

'Oh, but you have seen me often enough, Master Twig,' the wheedling voice continued. 'In the sleepy morning of the slaughterers' camp, in the sticky corridors of the gyle goblin colony, in the underground cavern of the termagant trogs . . . I was there. I was always with you.'

Twig went weak at the knees. He was confused, frightened. He racked his brains, trying to make sense of the words he was hearing. He *had* heard the soft insistent voice before, that much was certain. And yet . . .

'Can you really have forgotten, *Master* Twig,' came the voice again, and the air hissed with a nasal snigger.

Twig fell to his knees. The rock was cold and clammy to the touch; the mist grew thicker than ever. Twig could barely see his hand in front of his face. 'What do you want of me?' he whispered.

'Want of you? Want of YOU?' The voice broke into raucous laughter. 'It's what you want of *me*, Master Twig. After all, you did summon me.'

'I s . . . s . . . summoned you?' said Twig, the faltering words weak and muffled in the dense fog. 'But how? When?'

'Come, come,' the voice complained. 'Don't act the innocent little woodtroll with me. "Oh, Gloamglozer!" it said in a desperate voice that Twig recognized as his own. "*Please. Please. Please. Let me find the path again.*" Do you deny you called me?'

Twig trembled with horror as he realized what he'd done. 'But I didn't know,' he protested. 'I didn't mean . . .'

'You called me, and I came,' said the gloamglozer, and there was a menacing edge to the voice now. 'I followed you, I looked after you. More than once I led you out of the perilous situations you had got yourself into.' There was a pause. 'Did you not think that I was listening, Master Twig?' it went on, more gently now. 'I'm always listening: listening for the stragglers, the loners, the ones who don't fit in. I help, I guide, and eventually . . .'

'Eventually?' Twig murmured.

'They come to me,' the voice announced. 'As you have come to me, Master Twig.'

The mist thinned once more. It floated in the air like flimsy twists of cobweb. Twig discovered that he was kneeling next to the edge of a cliff. Inches away from him the ground fell away into pitch blackness. Behind him were the rolls of pungent cloud, and in front . . . Twig cried out in fear and alarm. In front, hovering over the void, was the hideous grinning face of the gloamglozer itself. Calloused and warty, with thick tussocks of hair sprouting out of its long snarling face, it leered at Twig and licked its lips.

'Come to me,' it coaxed. 'You called me and here I am. Take that final step, why don't you?' It held out a hand towards him. 'You belong with me.'

Twig stared back, unable to tear his gaze away from the creature's monstrous face. Two horns curled to thin sharp points; two yellow eyes fixed him in a hypnotic stare. The mist grew still thinner. Around the gloamglozer's shoulders was a greasy grey cloak which fell away into nothingness.

'One small step,' it said softly, and beckoned. 'Take my hand.' Twig stared down at the bony taloned fingers. 'That's all it takes – for someone like you, Master Twig – to join me,' the voice continued seductively, and the yellow eyes grew wide. 'For you are special.'

'*Special*,' Twig whispered.

'Special,' the gloamglozer repeated. 'I knew that from the moment I first heard your call. You had an overwhelming longing; an emptiness inside which you yearned to be filled. And I can help you. I can teach you. That's what you really want, isn't it, Master Twig? You want to know. To understand. *That's* why you left the path.'

'Yes,' said Twig dreamily. 'That's why I left the path.'

'The Deepwoods aren't for you,' the gloamglozer went on; flattering, insistent. 'Not for you the huddling together for safety, the hiding in corners, the fear of everyone and everything outside. Because you are like me. You're an adventurer, a traveller, a seeker. A listener!' Its voice became hushed and intimate. 'You too could be a gloamglozer, Master Twig. I can instruct you. Take my hand and you'll see.'

Twig moved a step closer. His ankle jarred. The gloam-glozer – still hovering in mid-air just beyond the Edge – trembled. Its monstrous face contorted with pain. Tears welled in the corners of its yellow eyes.

'Oh, what a time you've had of it,' it sighed. 'Constantly on the look-out. Never out of danger. Always frightened. But the tables can be turned, Master Twig. If you'll just *take my hand*.'

Twig shuffled awkwardly from one foot to the other. There was a rattle and a clatter as a flurry of dislodged rocks bounced down into the chasm. 'And look like *you*?' he said.

The gloamglozer threw back its head and roared with mirthless laughter. 'But have you forgotten, my vain little one?' it said. 'You can look how you will. A mighty warrior, a handsome prince ... Anything. Imagine it, Master Twig,' it went on enticingly. 'You could become a goblin or a trog,' and as it spoke Twig found himself face to face with a succession of characters he recognized only too well. There was the gyle goblin who had led him from the colony,

the flat-head who had helped him out of the mire,

the trog who had tripped Mag and pointed the way to
the air shafts.

'Or how about this one,' the gloamglozer purred. Twig
stared back at a red-faced individual with fiery hair.

'Didn't I hear you thinking how *nice* it would be to stay
with the slaughterers?' it wheedled. 'Or perhaps you'd
prefer to be a banderbear,' it said, shifting its shape
again. 'Big, powerful – no-one messes with a banderbear.' It sniggered unpleasantly. 'Except wig-wigs, of
course.'

Twig shuddered. The hovering creature knew everything. Absolutely everything.

'I've got it!' the gloamglozer cried, turning itself into a squat brown creature with knotted hair and a button nose.

'A woodtroll. You could go home. You could fit in. Isn't that what you wanted all along?'

Twig nodded his head mechanically.

'You can be *anyone*, Master Twig,' the gloamglozer said, resuming its own form. 'Anyone at all. You can go anywhere, do anything. Simply take hold of my hand, and all this shall be yours.'

Twig swallowed. His heart beat furiously. If the gloamglozer was right, he would never have to be an outsider again.

'And just think of the things you'll see,' the gloamglozer purred enticingly. 'Think of the places you could go, shifting your shape, appearing as others want to see you, always safe, listening in corners; always one step ahead. Think of the power at your command!'

Twig stared at the outstretched hand. He was standing at the very edge of the cliff. His arm moved slowly forwards, brushing against the spiky hammelhornskin waistcoat.

'Go on,' said the gloamglozer, its voice like oil and honey. 'Take that step forwards. Reach out and take my hand. You know you want to.'

Yet Twig still held back. It wasn't as if all his encounters in the Deepwoods had been bad. The banderbear had saved his life. So had the slaughterers. It was they, after all, who had given him the jacket that had caught in the bloodoak's gorge, which now bristled so sharply. He thought of his village and Spelda, his own dearest Mother-Mine, who had loved him like her own since the day that he was born. Tears welled up in his eyes.

If he accepted the gloamglozer's tantalizing offer, he would not really turn into them. No matter what I *look* like, he thought. Instead, he would become what they all feared most. A gloamglozer. No. It was impossible. He would never again be able to return. Never. He would have to remain apart, aloof – alone.

'It is fear which makes us reluctant to be on our own,' the gloamglozer said, reading his thoughts. 'Join me, and you need never be frightened again. Take my hand and you will understand. Trust me, Master Twig.'

Twig hesitated. Could this truly be the terrible monster that all the forest dwellers so feared?

'Have I let you down so far?' the gloamglozer asked quietly.

Twig shook his head dreamily.

'Besides,' it added, almost as an afterthought. 'I thought you *wanted* to see what lay beyond the Deepwoods.'

Beyond the Deepwoods. The three words rang round inside Twig's head. *Beyond* the Deepwoods. Twig held out his hand. He stepped over the edge.

With a screech of terrible laughter, the gloamglozer grabbed Twig's wrist, its talons biting into his flesh.

'They all fall for it,' the gloamglozer cried triumphantly. 'All the poor little goblins and trolls, waifs and strays; they *all* think they're special. They all listen to me. They all follow my voice . . . It's pathetic!'

'But you *said* I was special,' Twig cried, as he dangled from the gloamglozer's bony grasp over the yawning space below.

'Did I really?' the gloamglozer sneered. 'You little fool. Did you honestly think you could ever be like me?

You are as insignificant as all the rest, *Master* Twig,' it said scornfully. 'You are nothing. NOTHING!' it screeched. 'Do you hear me?'

'But why are you doing this?' Twig wailed desperately. 'Why?'

'Because I am a gloamglozer,' the beast cried out, and cackled wickedly. 'A deceiver, a trickster, a cheat and a fraud. All my fine words and fancy promises count for nothing. I seek out all those who have strayed from the path. I lure them to the Edge. AND I DISPOSE OF THEM!'

The gloamglozer released its grip. Twig screamed with terror. He was falling. Down, down, he went, over the Edge and into the bottomless depths of darkness below.

CHAPTER FOURTEEN

BEYOND THE
DEEPWOODS

Twig's head spun as he tumbled through the air. The uprush of wind set his clothes billowing and snatched his breath away. Over and over he rolled. And all the while, the gloamglozer's cruel words echoed round and round his head.

You are nothing. NOTHING!

'It's not true!' Twig howled.

The side of the cliff blurred past him like a streak of smudged paint. All that searching. All the trials and tribulations. All the times he had thought he would never make it to the end of the Deepwoods alive. To find his long lost father, only to lose him again – and then, worst of all, to discover that the whole treacherous journey had been a part of a cruel and complicated game devised by the deceitful gloamglozer. It was so, so monstrously unfair.

Tears welled in Twig's eyes. 'I'm *not* nothing. I'm not!' he wailed.

'I'm *not* nothing. I'm not!' Tears welled in his eyes.

Further and further he fell, down into the swirling mist. Would he fall for ever? He screwed his eyes shut.

'You're a liar!' Twig screamed back up to the top of the cliff.

Liar, liar, li . . . The word bounced back off the rock.

Yes, thought Twig, the gloamglozer *is* a liar. It lied about everything. Everything!

'I *am* something!' Twig called out. 'I am some*one*. I am Twig, who strayed from the path and travelled beyond the Deepwoods. I AM MEEEEEEE!'

Twig opened his eyes. Something had happened. He was flying, not falling, high above the Edge, in and out of clouds.

'Am I dead?' he wondered out loud.

'Not dead,' replied a familiar voice. 'Far from it. You still have far to go.'

'Caterbird!' cried Twig.

The caterbird's talons tightened their grip around Twig's shoulders; its great wings flapped rhythmically through the cold thin air.

'You were at my hatching, and I have watched over you always,' it said. 'Now you truly need me, here I am.'

'But where are we going?' asked Twig, who could see nothing but open sky.

'Not "we", Twig,' said the caterbird. 'But you. Your destiny lies beyond the Deepwoods.'

With that the talons released their grip and, for a second time, Twig was falling. Down, down, down and . . .

C R A S H !
Everything went black.

Twig found himself running down a long dark corridor. He dashed through a door into a dark room. In the corner was a wardrobe. He opened the door and stepped into the deeper darkness inside. He was looking for something; he knew that much. There was a coat hanging from a hook inside the wardrobe. Twig felt for the pocket, and climbed into the even deeper darkness inside. It wasn't here, whatever it was he was looking for, but there was a purse at the bottom. He opened the clasp and jumped into the even-deeper-still darkness within.

Inside the purse was a piece of cloth. Its touch was familiar. He felt the chewed and twisted corners. It was his scarf, his shawl. He picked it up and held it to his face, and there – staring back out of the darkness of the material – was a face. *His* face. It smiled. Twig smiled back.

'Me,' he whispered.

'Are you all right?' asked the face.

Twig nodded.

'Are you all right?' it said again.

'Yes,' said Twig.

The question came a third time, and Twig realized the voice was coming not from the scarf, but from somewhere else. Somewhere outside. His eyelids fluttered open. In front of him loomed a huge red hairy face. It looked concerned.

'Tem!' Twig exclaimed. 'Tem Barkwater.'

'The very same,' nodded the sky pirate. 'Now will you answer me – are you all right?'

'I . . . I think so,' said Twig. He pulled himself up onto his elbows. 'Nothing broken, at least.'

'How is he?' Spiker called.

'He's OK!' Tem shouted back.

Twig was lying on a soft bed of sailcloth on the deck of the sky ship. He pulled himself up and looked round. Apart from the Stone Pilot, they were all there: Spiker, Stope Boltjaw, Slyvo Spleethe, Mugbutt (chained to the mast), Hubble and, standing closest of all, the captain, Quintinius Verginix. Cloud Wolf. His father.

Cloud Wolf stooped and touched Twig's scarf. Twig flinched.

'Easy,' said the captain in a low voice. 'No-one's going to hurt you, lad. Seems we're not to be rid of you after all.'

'Never seen anything like it, cap'n,' broke in Tem Barkwater. 'Just dropped out of the sky, he did – straight onto the aft deck. This is strange sky we're in and no mistake . . .'

'Stop your chattering,' the captain said harshly. 'And get back to your posts, all of you. We must make Undertown by nightfall.'

The crew dispersed.

'Not you,' said the captain quietly, laying a hand on Twig's arm as he, too, made to leave.

Twig looked round. 'W . . . why did you leave me?' he asked, his mouth dry, his voice cracking.

The captain stared back, his mask-like face betraying no emotion. 'We didn't need an extra crew member,' he said simply. 'Besides, I didn't think that a pirate's life was for you.' He paused. There was clearly something weighing on his mind.

Twig stood there waiting for the captain to speak again. He felt shy, awkward. He chewed the inside of his mouth. The captain's eyes narrowed as he leaned forwards. Twig shuddered. The man's breath was warm and noisy at his ear, the side whiskers tickled his neck.

'I saw the shawl,' he confessed, so that only Twig could hear. 'Your scarf. The one that Maris – your mother – made. And I knew you were . . . After all those years.' He fell silent. His lower lip was trembling. 'It was more than I could bear. I had to get away. I . . . I left you behind. For a second time.'

Twig squirmed. His face was hot and red.

The captain placed his hands on Twig's shoulders and stared into his eyes. 'It will not happen a third time,' he said softly. 'I shall never abandon you again.'

He wrapped his arms around the boy and hugged him tightly. 'From now on our destinies lie together,' he whispered urgently, 'And you and I shall ride the skies together. You and I, Twig. You and I.'

Twig said nothing. He could not. Tears of joy welled in his eyes; his heart was beating ready to burst. He had found his father after all.

Abruptly, the captain pulled away. 'But you'll be a member of the crew, just like all the rest,' he added gruffly. 'So don't you go expecting any special favours.'

'No, f . . . captain,' said Twig quietly. 'I won't.'

Cloud Wolf nodded approvingly, straightened up and turned on the others, who had been watching, perplexed. 'Come on then, you idle rabble,' he roared. 'Show over. Raise the mainsail, lift the grappling rope, and let's get out of here.'

A chorus of 'aye-aye, cap'n's filled the air as the sky pirates set to work. The captain strode towards the helm with Twig beside him, and took the wheel.

Together at last, they stood side by side as the sky ship soared into the air and away, beyond the Deepwoods.

The captain turned towards his son. 'Twig,' he said thoughtfully, his eyes twinkling. '*Twig!* I mean, what kind of a name is that for the child of Quintinius Verginix, captain of the finest sky pirate ship that ever sailed the heavens blue? Eh? Tell me that.'

Twig smiled back. 'It's *my* name,' he said.